THE FORGOTTEN DOOR

Alexander Key

WITHDRAWN

AN
APPLE®
PAPERBACK

SCHOLASTIC INC.
New York Toronto London Auckland Sydney

No part of this publication may be reproduced in whole or in part, or stored in a retrieval system, or transmitted in any form or by any means, electronic, mechanical, photocopying, recording, or otherwise, without written permission of the publisher. For information regarding permission, write to The Westminster Press, Witherspoon Building, Philadelphia, PA 19107.

ISBN 0-590-40398-2

12 11 10 9 8 7 6 5 4 3 2 1   9   6 7 8 9/8 0 1/9

Printed in the U.S.A.   11

CONTENTS

To all those who like the starlight, and wonder about other places and other people.

He Is Lost and Found

IT HAPPENED SO QUICKLY, so unexpectedly, that Little Jon's cry was almost instantly cut short as the blackness closed over him. No one knew the hole was there. It hadn't been there the day before, and in the twilight no one had noticed it.

At the moment it happened, the first shooting stars were crossing the sky — they were beginning to stream across like strings of jewels flung from another planet — and everyone was watching them. The smaller children were exclaiming in delight, while the older ones stood silent and enthralled. Here on the hill, where the valley people often came to watch the glittering night unfold, you could see the whole magic sweep around you, and you felt close to everything in

1

the heavens. Other people, you knew, were standing on other hills on other worlds, watching even as you watched.

Little Jon, whose eyes were quicker than most, should have seen the hole, but all his attention was on the stars. Small for his age, he had moved away from the rest for a better view, and as he stepped backward, there was suddenly nothing under his feet.

It was astonishing at that moment to find himself falling swiftly into the hill at a spot where he had walked safely all his life. But in the brief seconds before the blackness swallowed him, he realized what must have happened: there had been a cave-in over the old Door — the Door that led to another place, the one that had been closed so long.

He cried out and tried to break his fall in the way he had been taught, but the effort came an instant too late. His head struck something, and darkness swirled over him.

Long later, when Little Jon was able to sit up, he had no idea where he was or what had happened. Memory had fled, and he ached all over. He would have been shivering with cold, but his thick jacket and trousers and heavy, woven boots kept him warm.

He seemed to be in a narrow cleft of broken rock. There were mossy stones around him, and just ahead

2

he could make out a bed of ferns where water trickled from a spring. He was still too dazed to be frightened, but now he realized he was thirsty, terribly so. He crawled painfully forward and lay with his face in the water while he drank.

The coldness of the water startled him at first, but it was wonderfully sweet and satisfying. He bathed his face and hands in it, then sat up at last and looked around again.

Where was he? How did he get here? He pondered these questions, but no answers came. He felt as if he had fallen. Only — where could he have fallen *from?* The rocky walls met overhead, sloping outward into a tangle of leafy branches.

There was another question his mind carefully tiptoed around, because it was more upsetting than the others. Whenever he approached it, it caused a dull aching in his forehead. Finally, however, he gave his head a small shake and faced it squarely.

Who am I?

He didn't know. He simply didn't know, and it made everything terribly wrong.

All at once, trembling, he got to his feet and fled limping toward a shaft of sunlight ahead. Thick shrubs barred his way. He fought blindly through them, tripped, and fell sprawling. Fortunately he missed the boulders on either side, and landed in a soft bed of old leaves under a tree. He scrambled up in panic,

3

started to run again, then stopped himself just in time.

This wasn't the sort of country where you could run. There were steep ledges here, and below them the ground sloped sharply downward for a great distance. All of it was covered with a wild tangle of forest. Little Jon rubbed his eyes and looked around him with growing wonder and fright.

Nothing here was familiar. He was *sure* of that. He had never seen trees quite like the ones around him. Many of the smaller trees were in bloom, covered with showers of white blossoms — these were *almost* familiar, as were the ferns and lichens on the rocks. But there was a difference. But what the difference was, he was unable to tell.

Carefully he worked down to an open area below the ledge, and stood listening. The *sounds* were familiar, and hearing them made him feel a bit better. Birdsong, the gurgling of hidden springs, the faint clatter and fuss of a rushing stream somewhere. And there were the hesitant steps of wild creatures that came pleasantly to his sharp ears. Without quite realizing his ability, which was as natural as breathing, his mind reached toward them and found nothing strange in them — except that they were afraid. Afraid of him!

"Don't be afraid," he told them, so softly that his lips barely moved. "I'd *never* hurt you."

After a minute, two of the creatures — they were

a doe and her fawn — moved hesitantly down the slope and stood looking at him curiously. Little Jon held out his hands, and presently the doe came close and nuzzled his cheek with her cold nose.

"Where am I?" he asked her plaintively. "Can you tell me?"

The doe couldn't answer, and all he could gather was that she was hungry, and that food could be found in the valley below.

"Lead the way," he told her. "I'll follow."

The doe and the fawn started down through the tangle. Little Jon went scrambling and limping behind them. Walking was difficult, for both his knees were badly bruised and one ankle pained with every step. Soon, however, they reached a winding game trail and the going was much easier. Even so, it was hard to keep up with the doe, and several times in the next hour he had to beg her to stop and wait for him.

It did not seem at all strange to be following her. Her presence was very comforting and kept the unanswered questions from troubling him.

As they wound down near the bottom of the slope, the trees thinned and they passed through an open gate. Ahead he could see bright sunlight on a small greening field. Around a corner of the field ran a clattering stream — a stream different from the one he had heard earlier.

At the sight of the field Little Jon caught his breath.

5

Fields and cultivated things were familiar. There would be people near. Soon he would meet them and find out about himself.

The doe paused at the edge of the field, sniffing the air currents. Little Jon could feel her uneasiness, though he could not understand it. He sniffed too, but all he could smell were the pleasant scents of fresh earth and blossoms, and the richness of the forest behind them. He was disappointed that he couldn't make out the scent of humans near, but maybe this was because the air was flowing down from the mountain, away from him.

As the doe stepped daintily into the field and began to nibble the young plants, Little Jon unconsciously did what he should have done earlier. His mind reached out, searching hopefully. He had no thought of danger. The sudden discovery that there *was* danger was so shocking that he could only spring forward with a strangled cry as he tried to tell the doe to run.

The doe whirled instantly and leaped, just as the sharp report of a rifle shattered the peace of the morning.

Little Jon had never heard a rifle shot before, but he was aware of the hot slash of pain across the doe's flank, and he could see the weapon in the hands of the man who rose from his hiding place at the edge of the stream. He was a lean man in overalls, with one shoulder higher than the other. The harsh features under the cap showed surprise and disbelief as he stared at Little Jon. Then the thin mouth twisted in fury.

"Devil take you!" the man roared, striding forward. "You ruint my aim! What you doin' in my field?"

Little Jon could make nothing of the words. The language was strange, but the hate-driven thoughts behind it were clear enough. For a moment he stood incredulous, his mind trying to fight through the shock of what had happened. Surely the man approaching was a being like himself. But why the intent to kill another creature? Why the sudden hate? How could anyone ever, ever . . .

The anger that rose in him was a new thing. It was something he had never experienced before, at least in this measure. His small hands balled into fists and he trembled. But just as quickly, he realized that he couldn't quench hate with hate, and that now there was danger to himself. He turned abruptly and fled.

"Stop!" the man bellowed, close behind him. "I know you — you're one o' them Cherokees from over the ridge! I'll teach you to come meddlin' on my land!"

Little Jon tried to lighten his feet and put distance between himself and his pursuer. Ordinarily he might have managed it in spite of his pains, but he knew nothing of barbed-wire fences. The rusty wires were hidden by the shrubbery until he was almost on them.

7

When he attempted to slide through them, the barbs caught his jacket. The tough material refused to tear. In another second he was squirming in the man's firm grasp.

The man dragged him roughly back to the field, then turned at the sound of an approaching motor. Presently a small farm truck whirled around the bend of the creek and stopped close by. A large woman, wearing faded overalls, got out and waddled over to them. She had a fleshy face, with small, shrewd eyes as hard and round as creek pebbles.

Little Jon had never seen a woman like her. Though he was repelled by her, she drew his attention far more than the truck, which was equally strange.

"I declare!" she muttered, staring. "What you got there, Gilby?"

"Not what I was aimin' at," the man growled. "The thievin' varmint spoiled my shot."

"Just as well, I reckon, or he'd tell. Whose kid is he?"

"Dunno, Emma. Figured 'im for a Cherokee, but —"

"Pshaw, *he* ain't no Indian," she interrupted, peering closer.

"Got black hair like one, near long as a girl's. Could be half an' half."

"H'mp! Look at them *clothes!* Seems more foreign-like. Gypsy, maybe. Where you from, boy?"

Little Jon clenched his teeth and looked stonily back at her. Though her speech was strange, the rising questions and ugly thoughts in her mind were easily understood. She was a person to be avoided, and he wouldn't have answered her even if he had known how.

"Cat got your tongue?" she snapped. "Well, I reckon I can loosen it." Abruptly she slapped him, hard.

He knew the slap was coming, and he managed in time to go limp and roll his head. As he did so, the man unclenched his hand to get a better grip on him. Immediately Little Jon twisted free and ran.

This time he was able to lighten his feet, and went over the fence in a bound. He heard gasps of astonishment behind him, then shouts, and the man's pursuing footsteps. Presently these sounds faded, and the forest was quiet.

Little Jon ran on until he was nearly exhausted. He would have followed the doe and the fawn, but they had gone over a ridge where the way was too steep for his throbbing ankle.

Finally he huddled by a fallen log, removed one boot, and rubbed his swollen ankle while he gained his breath. Tears rolled down his cheeks. He missed the doe terribly. She was his only friend in all this strangeness.

Suddenly he dug his knuckles into his eyes, drew on

his boot, and struggled to his feet. He couldn't stay here all day. It solved nothing. He had to keep moving, searching . . .

Resolutely he began limping around the curve of the slope, taking the easiest course. Somewhere there must be other people — people unlike those behind him. But when he found them he would have to be careful. Very careful.

He heard the soft slither of the snake ahead before he saw it, even before it rattled its deadly warning. Its sudden rattle astonished him. He stared at it with more curiosity than fear. What a strange creature, legless and covered with scales, and with a rattle on the end of its tail! It seemed he had heard of such things, vaguely, just as he had heard of the odd kind of vehicle the woman had driven. But where?

Troubled, he limped carefully around the snake. With the thought that there might be other dangers here, dangers he knew nothing about, he drew a small knife from his belt and cut a staff from the shrubbery. The knife felt so much a part of him that he hardly questioned it till he had finished using it. It was only a tool — it seemed that someone had given it to him long ago — but he couldn't remember any more about it.

The staff made walking easier for a while, and he trudged painfully on, stopping at times to rest or to drink from one of the many springs. The sun, which he could glimpse only at intervals through the trees, began to sink behind him. He was very hungry, and his eyes searched continually for food. There ought to be berries. He had noticed some earlier, growing near the barbed-wire fence where the man had caught him.

Edible things, he decided finally, must grow in the open places, lower down.

Warily, slowly, he began to angle toward the valley. He reached the bottom of the slope much sooner than he had expected, only to discover that the valley had vanished. Another slope rose immediately ahead. In sudden alarm he realized he could no longer see the sun. With every step the gloom was deepening. The forest had chilled, and for the first time he saw the gray mist creeping down from above.

The gloom, the chill, and the creeping mist in this strange and bewildering land, together with his growing hunger and lameness, were almost too much. A sob broke from his lips, and he began to tremble with a black dread. He couldn't go much farther. What would he do when darkness came?

Then, like a glow of warmth in the chill, he felt the comforting knowledge of wild creatures near. They were friendly, but timid. He was on the point of calling to them when he heard the distant sound of a motor. He stiffened, his hands clenched tightly on his staff. Memory of the angry man and the ugly woman rose like a warning. He shook off the thought of them.

He *had* to go on. It was the only way . . .

Abruptly he began plunging toward the sound, following the narrow gully that curved away on his right.

A half hour later he broke through a tangle of evergreens and stared in amazement at the scene ahead.

He was on the edge of a steep bank that dropped down to a winding gravel road. Beyond the road a broad valley opened. The valley was ringed by wave on wave of blue and purple mountains that rose to the clouds. The valley was in shadow, but he could make out the farms with their little white houses, and see animals grazing in the pastures.

The motor he had heard earlier had passed, but a second one was approaching. Instantly his mind went out to it, exploring. There were several people in the vehicle, and they were very different from the ones he had met — but not different in a way that mattered. As the machine swung into sight, he allowed himself only a curious glimpse of its bright newness, before he cowered back into the tangle.

The shadows deepened in the valley, and began to creep over the distant mountains. Three more vehicles passed, and once a man on a horse went by. The horse sensed his presence and whinnied. Little Jon liked the horse, but he fought down the urge to call to it, for the man filled him with uneasiness.

It was nearly dark when he heard the final motor. This time, aware of the friendliness of its occupants

— and something beyond friendliness — he did not hesitate. It was a small truck, and as it swung around the bend in the road, he slipped quickly down the bank to meet it.

He Gains a Home

As HIS BOOTS struck the edge of the road, his bad ankle
gave way under him, and Little Jon fell in a heap. For
a moment he was afraid the truck would go past without anyone noticing him. Its headlights were on, but
the beams were sweeping beyond him around the
curve.

He managed to struggle upright for a moment, then
sank weakly to his knees. He had dropped his staff,
and found that he could hardly stand without it.

The truck braked suddenly, and stopped. A man
leaned out and said in quick concern, "Hey there,
young fellow! What seems to be wrong?"

Little Jon opened his mouth soundlessly, and raised
one hand. He heard a woman's voice say, "For heav-

14

en's sake, children, let me out — I think the boy's hurt!"

Both doors of the truck flew open. The man stepped from the driver's side, and a boy and a girl tumbled from the other, followed by the woman. Little Jon saw that the girl was about his own size. The boy was much larger, but he seemed no older than himself. Both wore jackets and blue jeans, like the woman.

Though the man was nearer, he moved with a slight limp, and the woman reached him first. "My goodness, honey," she said, stooping and raising him gently, "your face and hands are all scraped. Did you have a fall?"

He nodded, and the man asked, "Are you hurt badly?"

Little Jon shook his head. His eyes swung quickly from one to the other. The woman wore a green scarf around her bright hair. There were freckles across her lean cheeks, and small laughter creases at the corners of her eyes and mouth. The man had a thick shock of dark hair graying at the temples; his face was ruddy, but deeply lined.

The man said, "Can you tell us where you live, sonny?"

Little Jon shook his head again. There was sudden silence. The woman bit her lip, then asked quietly, "Can you understand what we are saying?"

Again he nodded, and she said, "Thomas, I believe

15

he's had a bad shock that keeps him from speaking. I — I hate to take him to the hospital. They — they're so impersonal. I think all he needs is a hot meal and some rest."

"We're taking him home with us," the man said definitely. "If he's been lost in the mountains all day, he's had it." He jerked his head at the boy and girl. "Sally, you and Brooks ride in the back of the truck. Mary — "

"I'll carry him," she said. "He hardly weighs what Sally does."

"Mommy," said Sally, speaking for the first time. "Is — is he an Indian?"

"I doubt it, and it wouldn't make any difference if he were a horned Andalusian with scales. All aboard!"

She swung Little Jon into the truck and settled him on the seat beside her. The two children scrambled into the back, and the man slid behind the wheel.

While the truck wound along the road, Little Jon sat with his hands clenched, trying to suppress the sudden tears of thankfulness that ran down his cheeks. It was so wonderful to find people who were, well, like people should be. If only he could talk to them and explain . . .

He tried to fit their spoken words to the thoughts he had felt in them. Their names he knew: Thomas, Mary, Sally, Brooks. His quick ears had already picked out scores of words for his eager memory to hold, but fitting them to the right thoughts would take time. He

16

wished they would speak more to one another, but they said little during the short drive.

Even so, he was aware of questions in all of them. The man: *Odd — never saw a boy like him. Can't be from around here.* The woman: *There's something very strange about him. It isn't just his long hair. His features are so — so sensitive. And his jacket — where in the world can you find material like that?*

The truck slowed presently, and the headlights swept a small brown building with a sign that read BEAN'S ROCK SHOP, SMOKY MOUNTAIN GEMS. The truck turned into a lane beside it, and climbed in second gear to a house nearly hidden by evergreens. There was a barn some distance behind the house, and Little Jon was aware of animals there, waiting. A dog barked furiously at them until he gave it an answering thought of friendliness.

They got out, and the woman carried him to the door, which the man opened with a key. Lights came on, and he was placed on a couch by a fireplace. It was a comfortable room, paneled in brown wood. He was aware of a flicker of pride in the man, who had built this home with his own hands.

The man said, "Brooks, you and Sally unload the groceries, then look after the stock."

"Aw, Dad," Brooks grumbled. "Please, can't we — "

"Do as I say, and I'll handle the milking later. There'll be plenty of time to get acquainted with him.

17

And if your mother will whip up some supper for us, I'll build a fire and play doctor. This boy needs attention."

While the man kindled a fire, Little Jon removed his woven boots and carefully rolled his trousers above his knees.

The man, turning, saw the bruises and whistled softly. He examined them carefully. "You sure got banged up, young fellow, but I don't believe any bones are broken. Some of the Bean family liniment ought to do the trick. Good for everything from hornet stings to housemaid's knee."

At that moment, as Brooks and his sister were bringing in the last of the groceries, a truck turned into the lane outside. Little Jon sat up quickly, his lips compressed. There was no mistaking the particular sound of that truck.

Brooks peered out of the window. "I think it's Mr. Gilby Pitts, Dad."

Thomas Bean frowned. "Wonder what Gilby — " He stopped, and exclaimed, "Hey, young fellow, what's come over you?"

Little Jon was on his feet, trembling, trying to limp away. It was not fear that made him tremble, but a sudden return of the morning's shock, when he had met an evil that was beyond his understanding.

Mary Bean, entering from the kitchen, put her arm

18

around him and asked softly, "Have you had trouble with Mr. Pitts, dear?"

At his tight face and nod, she frowned at her husband. "Thomas, he's afraid of Gilby. I don't know what's happened, but I don't like — "

"Take him into our bedroom and close the door," Thomas Bean said quickly. "Knowing Gilby, I'd just as soon not — "

Save for the forgotten boots near the sofa, the room was clear when the knock sounded.

After an exchange of greetings, Gilby Pitts entered. "You folks just git home, Tom?" he asked.

"Oh, a short while ago."

"See anything kinda unusual on the way back?"

"Saw a nice sunset. Why?"

"H'mp! I don't pay no mind to sunsets." Gilby shuffled toward the fireplace, rubbing his unshaven jaw against his high shoulder. His narrow eyes darted about the room. "There's queer things goin' on around here, Tom. I don't like it. You still got that bloodhound you raised?"

"No. Traded it to Ben Whipple over at Windy Gap for a calf. Trying to train another dog, but he's a tough one. About got me licked."

"Sure wish you had that hound. I got a mind to go over to Whipple's an' borrow him."

"What on earth for?" Thomas Bean looked at Gilby curiously.

"Might as well tell you, Tom. There's a wild boy loose in this country. Seen 'im with my own eyes. Emma can tell you. I caught the little varmint, but Emma an' me couldn't git nothin' out of him. While we were tryin' to make 'im talk, he tore loose an' took off like a streak. Never seen nothin' like it! Cleared a fence like — like — "

"A wild boy!" Thomas exclaimed. Then he asked softly, "What was he doing when you caught him, Gilby?"

"Trespassin'. An' I got signs up. I — "

"Oh, come now. No one worries about trespassing signs except in hunting season. You know that. We cross each other's land all the time. Saves miles of travel by the roads. I do it all the time when I'm out rock-hunting."

"This is a heap different. I been missing things. I — "

"Did it ever occur to you," Thomas Bean interrupted, "that this boy you're talking about could be lost, and in need of help? Why, he could be badly hurt — "

"*He* weren't hurt! You shoulda seen 'im jump!"

"Then you must have frightened him badly. Why did you frighten him?"

"The varmint come sneakin' down to that west field o' mine with the deer. He — "

"With the *deer!*"

"That's what I said. *With the deer.* Just like he was one of 'em!"

Thomas pursed his lips, then said dryly, "You wouldn't have been taking a shot at one, would you, Gilby?"

Gilby Pitts spat angrily into the fireplace. "Fool deer been ruinin' my field. Man's got a right to scare 'em away."

"But the boy —"

"He took off, an' got tangled in the barbed-wire fence, or I'd never acaught 'im. Acted like he didn't know the barbed wire was there. But he knowed it the second time, when he busted loose. Sailed right over it like he had wings. I tell you he's wild. Wild as they come." Gilby stopped. In a lower tone he added, "An' that's not all. *He ain't natural.* I don't like *unnatural* things around. If there's more like 'im, we ought to know about it."

There was a moment's silence. In the adjoining bedroom, where every word of the conversation could be heard, Mary Bean had opened the liniment bottle and was rubbing Little Jon's bruises. There was wonder in her eyes as she whispered, "Is that true about the deer? You were — friendly with them?"

He nodded, and struggled to fit new words to thoughts. But the words were too few.

"You're an odd one," she whispered. "I wish you could remember your name. Try real hard."

"J — Jon," he said. The name came unbidden to his lips. There was more to it, but the rest would not come.

They fell silent, for Thomas Bean was talking.

"Gilby," said Thomas, "if I were you, I'd go sort of easy about this. Suppose a stray kid from over at the government camp got lost. If he fell and hurt himself, he could wander around in a daze, not even knowing who he was. If you actually found him, and scared him away instead of trying to help him, you'd be in for a lot of criticism."

"Well, mebbe . . ."

"What's more, this isn't hunting season, and you'd be in for more trouble if people thought you were trying to sneak some venison."

"Now lissen to me, Tom —"

"I'm only telling you the truth, Gilby. Anyway, it's quite possible that some Cherokee boys from the Reservation came over this way on a hike. You know how they are in the spring."

"Aw, I dunno. Emma didn't think he was no Cherokee." Gilby shuffled around, and suddenly muttered, "I declare. Them's queer-lookin' boots yonder."

In the bedroom, Mary Bean stood up quickly, alarm in her blue eyes. She went to the door and started to slip into the hall, but at that instant Sally darted past her from the kitchen.

"Hello, Mr. Gilby," Sally chirped brightly, scooping

the boots from under Gilby Pitt's nose. "My goodness, Mommy will scalp me if I don't get the mud off these." She skipped back into the kitchen, calling, "Mommy, when are we going to have supper? I'm *hungry!*"

"Coming in a minute, dear," her mother answered.

Gilby Pitts scowled, rubbed his chin on his high shoulder, and finally shambled toward the door. "Reckon I'll be goin', Tom. Let me know if you hear anything."

"Sure will. Be seeing you."

No one said a word until Gilby Pitts's truck was safely down the road. Then Thomas expelled a long breath. "Confounded old skinflint!" he muttered.

"Do you think he suspected anything?" Mary said, bringing Little Jon back into the room.

"Probably not. He's just nosy. I only wish he hadn't seen the boy this morning — but maybe I've calmed him down enough so he won't do anything." He grinned suddenly at his daughter. "Thanks, Sally, for snatching the boots. That was quick thinking."

"I deserve a dime for that," Sally said pertly, holding out her hand. "Fork over!" she demanded. "Don't be a stingy-puss."

"Mercenary wretch," he growled, giving her the dime. He stooped and kissed her.

"I'm *not* mercenary," she said. "See, I can give as well as receive." She pressed the dime into Little Jon's hand. "It's yours — and — and I hope you stay with us a *long* time."

Brooks Bean, who had temporarily forgotten his chores, watched the exchange with interest. Abruptly he burst out, "Say, guy, didn't you ever see a dime before?"

"His name is Jon," said Mary Bean. "Like short for Jonathan. His name is all he can remember at the moment."

"But — but, jumping smoke," Brooks persisted, "a dime's a dime. Don't you know what money is, Jon?"

Little Jon shook his head.

"But you must know English, or you wouldn't know what we're saying," Brooks went on, baffled. "So you must know about *money!*"

Mary Bean said firmly, "We've questioned him enough for one evening. After all, if you had a bump on your head as big as his, you wouldn't know which way was up. Jon's had a pretty bad day. What he needs is something to eat, and a good night's rest. Tomorrow's Sunday, and there'll be plenty of time to talk."

There was only one other surprise that evening. They had scrambled eggs for supper, along with some of Mary Bean's home-canned vegetables, generous slices of baked ham, and some fried chicken left over from the day before. Little Jon ate ravenously of everything but the ham and chicken, which he refused to touch.

He began to nod at the table, and was sound asleep before he could finish undressing for bed. He shared Brooks's bed that night and wore a pair of old pajamas, much too large for him, that Brooks had outgrown.

He Learns a New Language

IN THE MORNING little Jon felt nearly as well as ever. Save for the bump on his head, which was better, all his swellings had gone down during the night, and the ugly bruises had almost vanished. There was hardly a sign of the scratches that had marred his hands and face. He could walk easily.

"I can't understand it," Mary Bean said at breakfast. "I *never* saw anyone heal so fast. I've heard of fast healers, but . . ."

"Oh, it's only our special Bean liniment," Thomas said lightly, carefully hiding his own surprise. "Jon, it's an old Indian concoction. Supposed to cure everything but poverty and rabies. If it wasn't for the poverty restriction, I could sell it in the shop and make a fortune on it."

"Aw, Dad," Brooks began, but Sally said brightly, "Why don't we rub some on Jon's head? Maybe it would bring back his memory!"

Little Jon laughed. He knew she meant it, which made it all the funnier.

The others laughed with him, then looked at him curiously.

Thomas Bean said, "It's good to hear you laugh, Jon. That means your voice will be coming back soon as well as your memory. Then we can locate your folks." He paused, frowning. "What I can't understand is why there was no mention of you on the radio this morning. Ordinarily, in this mountain country, if anyone gets lost, you hear about it first thing on the local station and search parties go out. But there wasn't a word."

Mary Bean murmured, "I hope it wasn't like what happened over beyond the gap last summer."

Brooks said, "Jon, some tourists drove off the mountain, but nobody even knew about it for a week. Some hikers just happened to stumble over their car. Everybody in it was stone dead."

"Brooks!" his mother said despairingly. "You shouldn't —"

"Aw, *he* didn't wander off from any wrecked car," Brooks told her. "I know. I asked him about it while we were getting dressed. Jon doesn't know any more about cars than he does about money."

Thomas Bean blinked. "Is that true, Jon?"

"Yes," said Little Jon, speaking his first word of English.

"He spoke!" Sally cried, delighted. "Maybe some of the liniment got on his tongue."

Neither Thomas nor Mary laughed. They glanced at each other, their eyes shadowed with questions. Mary Bean said, "Thomas, I'm not going to church this morning. Why don't you go on with Brooks and Sally, and sort of nose around . . ."

"Um, O.K. I follow you. I'll see what I can pick up — without saying anything."

"Right. Now, Brooks," she said, "you and Sally listen to me carefully. I don't want either of you to mention a word about Jon to a soul. Understand?"

"Yes, ma'am," said Brooks. "I'm not dumb."

"But why shouldn't we mention him?" Sally asked. "I think Jon's *nice*, don't you?"

"Of course he is, dear. And we want to protect him. Remember how Mr. Gilby was last night?"

"Oh, *him!*" Sally wrinkled her nose in distaste.

"So you see how it is, dear. There are too many things about Jon that people like Mr. Gilby can't understand — and they could make all kinds of, well, difficulties. Will you promise to keep Jon a secret?"

"I promise, Mommy."

"That's my girl," said Thomas, smiling at her. "Better get ready, you two. We don't want to be late."

28

When they were gone, Mary Bean went to the radio and tuned it carefully to the local station. She listened to the next news report, then shook her head.

"Do you know about radios?" she asked.

Little Jon was not deceived by the casual tone of her voice. The question was important to her, for behind it were those troubling thoughts about cars and money.

"Yes," he replied. Then he remembered the politeness word, and said, "Yes, ma'am."

"Wonderful!" she exclaimed. "It's coming back. Is it hard to talk?"

"It is hard — now. But — it is coming." He liked her bright hair, and her quick blue eyes that were almost green. Sally looked much like her, but Brooks resembled his father.

"Well, we'll take it easy," she said. "Maybe I shouldn't talk to you at all for a day or two. You may have a concussion or something — I don't know too much about those things, but you've still got that bump on your head. Does it hurt this morning?"

"Only — when I — touch it. Please — talk. It — helps."

"O.K. We'll talk up a storm. I'm the biggest talker in seven counties — when I have the chance." She laughed. "Poor Thomas is too busy trying to keep the money coming in to listen to me half the time."

"Money?" he said. "Why?"

"There we go again! Money. You *must* know what

money is! Everybody has to have it. You can't eat without it — though we manage pretty well, what with a
garden and the stuff I can from it, plus chickens and a
cow. They call this place a farm — but no farmer
could possibly make a living from it these days, no
matter how hard he worked. And we all work hard.
Thomas is no farmer — but he refuses to live in cities,
so he studied geology after the war, and managed to
buy this place and start the Rock Shop. That's where
our money comes from — mainly during the summer
from tourists."

She stopped, her eyes crinkling. "Am I talking too
much?"

"Oh, no! Please — please talk more."

"All right. About money. Are you absolutely certain
you've never seen any before?"

"Absolutely certain."

"And the same for automobiles?"

"They are — strange to me."

"And you're getting stranger to me by the minute."

Mary Bean sat down, and he was aware of her growing bewilderment as she stared at him. His own bewilderment matched hers, but he fought it down while
his mind sorted the dozens of new words he was learning. Words were used in patterns, and they had to
match the patterns that thoughts came in. It was very
easy — but it took time.

Suddenly she jumped up. "Jon, I'm going through

the house and point out things. I want you to tell me whether they are familiar or strange. You know about radios, so you should know about TV also."

"It is like radio — but has — pictures?"

"Yes, television. We don't have a set — we've been using our extra money for books — but we hope to get one soon."

"Television — it seems familiar."

"Good. What about books?" She waved to the shelves of books flanking the fireplace.

"Familiar," he said instantly.

"Can you read this one?" She handed him a copy of one of Sally's books.

"No. I cannot read — this."

"That's strange. I get the feeling you're older than you look. Anyone who speaks English ought to be able to read this. Oh, dear, I didn't realize — maybe English isn't your language."

"There *is* another language I — I seem to know."

"Now we're getting somewhere!" she exclaimed happily. "If you could speak a little of it, maybe I could recognize it."

Little Jon looked out of the window, and let his mind rove over the greening valley in the distance. Suddenly he began to hum a little song about valleys. The humming changed to singing words. He wondered where he had heard it.

Mary Bean clapped her hands. "That was beautiful,

Jon! Beautiful!" Her bewilderment returned. "I
thought I knew something about languages — my
father taught them in school. But this is a new one.
How long have you known English?"

"I don't know it yet. I only began — last night."

She shook her head. "Say that again?"

"I — I am learning it from you, now," he said, and
instantly wondered if he should have told her. She
didn't believe him. It was strange that she couldn't
understand thoughts, even strong ones — but nobody
here seemed to be able to. Only the animals . . .

"Jon," she said, very patiently, "do you know the
difference between truth and — and falsehood?"

"Truth? Falsehood? Truth is — is right," he managed to say. "Falsehood is — not truth. There is another word for it — but you have not spoken it yet."

"The word is 'lie,'" she said softly. "When you are
not telling the truth, you are telling a falsehood — a
lie."

His chin quivered a moment, then stiffened. "You
think I am not telling you the truth — but — but I
must! You are as strange to me as — as I am to you.
Yesterday — in the morning — I woke up — on a
mountain — far away from — from here. I hurt all
over. I felt as if — as if I had fall — fallen. I did not
know my name until last night, when you asked me.
Everything was strange. The mountain, the trees,

32

everything . . . only the deer. I — " He stopped, all
at once aware of the dog he had glimpsed last night.

The dog was thirsty. It was almost a hurt to feel the
dryness of its throat, the craving for water.

He told Mary Bean about the dog, but she shook
her head. "Oh, I'm sure he was taken care of. Thomas
wouldn't forget Rascal. Anyway, how could you possibly — "

"But he *did* forget the water. How could Rascal
think a lie?"

"Jon!" There was something like fright in her eyes.
"Are you trying to tell me that you can — " She shook
her head, and said, "We'll go out to Rascal's pen and
see — "

They had started through the doorway when they
heard a car coming down the road. Instantly she drew
him back inside and closed the door. They stood waiting for the car to pass. It slowed, then went on.

"The Johnsons," she said. "They would have stopped
if they'd seen us. Thank goodness they didn't."

Almost in the same breath she said firmly, "Rascal
will have to wait. Jon, I'm going to cut your hair, and
I'm going to give you some different clothes to wear.
I hope you don't mind, but I want you to look as much
like other boys as possible. It's terribly important."

"I don't mind," he said, giving Rascal a quieting
thought. "I'm sorry to — to make so much trouble."

"I don't mind it in the least. In fact, if I can only get used to you, I believe I'm going to enjoy this. But getting used to you . . ."

She got scissors and a comb, and started to cut. She found the nearly hidden clip holding his hair together at the nape of his neck. "O-o-oh!" she gasped. "What workmanship! Thomas will be interested in this."

She put the clip carefully aside, and very expertly cut his hair. "I'm the family barber," she explained. "You'd be surprised what it saves. Costs a dollar-fifty in town, and nearly double that in cities. That's six dollars a month for Brooks and Thomas. Now, let's see. Clothes. Most of Brooks's old things went to the charity collection, but I saved the best for Sally to play in. They ought to fit you."

When he was finally dressed in faded jeans, a fairly good shirt, and a light zipper jacket, she surveyed him critically.

"We're short on shoes," she said, "but I think your boots will pass, if you keep your trousers pulled over them. Next, we've got to think up a story to explain your presence here. I know — Thomas had a pal in the Marines named Jimmy O'Connor. He married a French-Moroccan girl when he was stationed in North Africa. They were both killed in the trouble there recently — so who's to know if they didn't have a son about your age? You do look, well, a bit foreign. I don't see why we couldn't call you Jon O'Connor, and say we'd sort of fallen heir to you for the time being."

"But — but that would not be truth," he said, wondering.

"Oh, dear, there we go again." She sighed, and sat down, frowning. "Jon, in this day and age, with the way things are, truth — the exact truth — is often a hard thing to manage. There are times when it could cause needless trouble and suffering."

"Things must be — very wrong if — if truth can cause trouble," he replied simply.

She sighed again. "You're probably right — but that's the way the world is. Even in little things, we often tell white lies to save people's feelings."

"White lies?"

"Well, take Mrs. Johnson. She makes her own clothes, just as I do. But she's never learned to sew well, and she makes the ugliest dresses in the community. Still, I wouldn't hurt her feelings by telling her how ugly they are. I usually think of something nice to say about them."

Little Jon was puzzled. "But that's not right. How can she learn? It's wrong to make things ugly. Why, if she's wrong, should her feelings — "

"Oh, Jon! I don't understand you!" She shook her head. "Listen, dear. To avoid trouble, I'm afraid you'll have to be Jimmy O'Connor's boy — until we can find out more about you. I don't dare tell the Johnsons, or the Pitts, or some other people, that — that you're a strange boy from nowhere, who has curious clothes that won't tear, and curious ideas that don't fit, who has never seen money or cars before, and who can talk to — " She stopped, and again he was aware of the flicker of fright in her mind.

Quietly she said, "Let's go out and see if Rascal really is thirsty."

Rascal was a huge brown mongrel, with a wide head and heavy jaws. He snarled as they approached the enclosure, and lunged to the end of his chain. The iron pan that held water was empty. Mary Bean frowned at the pan. She turned on the hose and filled it from a safe distance. Rascal quieted and drank greedily.

"How you ever knew about that pan — " she began. "Anyway, I'd better warn you about Rascal. Thomas is always picking up stray dogs and trying to train them — but this creature was a mistake. He won't let anyone but Thomas go near him. We've got to get rid of him. If he ever broke that chain . . ."

"He — he won't hurt you."

"I happen to know better. He's as vicious as they come, and even Thomas — No! *Don't open that gate!*"

He hardly heard her, for he had slipped quickly through the gate and all his attention was on Rascal. He held out his hands, and the big dog came over to him, uncertain, then whining in sudden eagerness, trembling. As he spoke silently he could feel the blackness and the lostness fade away from the brooding creature that now sprang happily upon him.

Thomas Bean, returning, glimpsed the two from the foot of the lane. He sent the truck roaring up to the house and jumped out, calling, "Hey, you crazy kid! Get out of there before — "

His voice died with recognition. Shaken, he limped over to Mary, followed by Brooks and Sally. "Didn't know him with a haircut and those clothes," he muttered. "Lord preserve me, how did he *ever* make up to Rascal?"

"I'll try to tell you later," she whispered, "but you won't believe it. Incidentally, I've decided that he's Jimmy O'Connor's boy. We — we've got to explain him somehow."

Thomas nodded slowly. "Jimmy O'Connor is a good choice. Be hard for anyone to check up on it."

"Did you learn anything at church?"

"Not a thing. I was surprised to see Gilby and Emma there. They don't belong to our church."

"They must have come with the Macklins — they're related, you know."

"Well, the Macklins were all there. They sang as loud as anybody — and they looked well fed on Bean hams."

"Thomas! You don't actually *know* that they stole our hams last fall."

"No, I certainly couldn't prove it. Anyway, I drove through town afterward, listened around a bit, and got all the papers I could find. Atlanta *Journal*, Asheville *Times*, and a couple others. There's bound to be something in one of them about a lost boy."

"Want to make a bet on it?"

"But, Mary, he had to come from *somewhere!*"

Little Jon called from the enclosure, "Please, may — may I take Rascal out? He — he hates the chain."

"Why, say, you're getting your voice back!" Thomas exclaimed. "You're really progressing, young fellow. Er, I don't know how you made up to Rascal, but I think you'd better leave him where he is."

"He — he promises to be good."

"Oh, he *promises*, does he?" Thomas chuckled. "Well, some dogs can break promises the way people do. Maybe, tomorrow . . ."

Little Jon turned away to hide his disappointment. *He doesn't understand,* he silently told Rascal. *But he will. Be patient, and tomorrow we will play together.*

He heard Thomas say to Mary, "Thank heaven he's able to talk to us. Seems like a pretty bright kid, so it shouldn't be too hard to find out a few facts about him."

"Thomas," Mary whispered, "I have something to tell you about his speech. Get a double grip on yourself and come into the house."

He Makes a Discovery

THE NEXT MORNING, as soon as Brooks and Sally had gone to meet the school bus, Thomas Bean said, "Let's all get down to some facts and see what we can figure out."

A study of the papers had yielded not the slightest clue, and it had been decided to save all further questions until this time, when they would have the morning to themselves. Little Jon had looked forward hopefully to this moment, yet he approached it with misgivings. His memory still told him nothing. And the Beans, much as he was beginning to love them, were still as strange to him as he was to them.

"Let's start with your clothes," said Thomas, limping over to the table on which Mary had placed them. "They should tell us a lot. Is everything here?"

"All but my boots — and my knife and belt," he said. "I'm still wearing them."

Mary Bean said, "His boots are woven of the same material as the rest of his clothes, only thicker. Even the soles."

"No leather?" said Thomas.

"Thomas," she said, "there isn't a scrap of leather in anything he owns."

"Leather" was a new word. Little Jon asked about it, and was shocked when he learned. "But how — how can you kill another creature for its skin?" he exclaimed.

"That's the way people live, young fellow," Thomas said, frowning as he wrote something on a piece of paper. "Well, that's another odd fact about you. I'm going to stop being surprised, and just jot down the facts. I learned in the Marines that if you get enough facts together, no matter how queer they may look alone, they'll always add up to something."

The pencil in Thomas Bean's hand moved swiftly as he intoned, "No leather. Doesn't believe in killing things. Will not eat meat. Seems to know how to — to communicate with animals. H'mm. Clothes, all hand-woven. Material like linen . . ."

"It's a hundred times stronger than linen," Mary hastened to say. "The soles of his boots hardly show a sign of wear."

"Vegetable fiber," Thomas mumbled, writing.

"Tougher than ramie. Dove gray. Designs on hem of jacket in tan and blue. Could be Indian or Siberian —"

"But they're not," said Mary Bean, "and I don't see any sense in writing all that down when I know the answer."

"And what *is* the answer, Madame Bean?"

"I — I'm not ready to tell you," she said. "You should be seeing it for yourself. I think Jon sees it. Do you, Jon?"

He was startled by her thought. "You could be right," he told her slowly. "I almost believe you are — but I'm not sure yet. You're better able to judge. You have your memory."

"Hey, what's all this?" Thomas asked curiously.

"Skip it," Mary told him. "You're the fact finder. Have you listed his English as one of the facts?"

"I'm listing it as a language that he knows."

"That's not what I mean, Thomas."

"Oh, come on. It takes years to learn English the way he speaks it. Jon's picked it up somewhere — he'd forgotten it temporarily. That crack on the head —"

"No," said Little Jon. "Your language is new to me. I'm sure I never heard it until you spoke it. But I find it — easy."

"Oh, I don't doubt your word," said Thomas Bean, "but English just *seems* strange to you. There isn't a living soul who can pick it up in a day or two. That's

41

absolutely impossible. The thing is, you're able to sort of know our thoughts before we speak them. That's an unusual ability — though I've heard of people who can do it. Anyway, it's an ability that's helping you to relearn English as fast as you hear it. Doesn't that sound right to you?"

Little Jon shook his head. "No, sir. I — I don't *think* in English. There's another language I — "

"We'll come to that in a minute. It's all adding up."

"What about cars and money?" Mary Bean asked quickly. "Can you add those up with the rest of it?"

"Certainly," said Thomas. He was pacing back and forth with his awkward step, one hand rubbing his deeply lined face while he frowned at his notes. "It's beginning to make sense. Even the fact that he knows about radios, and nothing about some other things. How's this:

"Jon was raised in a foreign country, in a very remote district. He learned to speak the language of that district — probably before he learned English. Because it was a primitive sort of place, there was no money, and all trade was by barter. Naturally there'd been no cars there. But his folks had a radio so they could keep in touch with the outside world. Wouldn't be surprised if his folks were missionaries. Sound right to you?"

Mary said, "Why must you be so — so reasonable, Thomas? But go ahead. Name some places like that."

"Oh, that's easy. I've been in a number of them. Parts of India, the Middle East, North Africa, and even South America. Those clothes could have been woven by Indians in the Andes."

"Nonsense," Mary said. "Those people weave only with animal fibers and cotton. The material in Jon's clothes didn't come from any of the places you mentioned."

"Well, where *did* it come from?"

"Not from any place you know about — and while you're thinking of places, you might consider *how* he got here. That really stumps me."

"He must have flown, Mary."

"In what kind of plane, Thomas?"

"Oh, a small private one, I'd say — one that hasn't been missed yet. It *has* to be that. There's no other solution. You see, when we found him he was still wearing the clothes he must have put on when he left home. He'd hardly be wearing such odd-looking things if he had been in this country long enough to change them. I wish I'd thought of this earlier! He must have come in a plane, and it must have crashed somewhere here in the mountains. We'd better organize a search — "

Mary was shaking her head. "No, Thomas. Jon has never seen a plane in his life. He saw pictures of some in one of our magazines yesterday, and asked me what they were."

Thomas stared at her, then turned. "Is that true, Jon?"

"Yes, sir. I'm certain I've never been in a plane, Mr. Bean."

"But your memory, Jon —"

"My lost memory doesn't keep me from knowing familiar things," he said earnestly.

"H'mm. Well, what *is* familiar to you?"

"Radios are familiar, sir. Books are very familiar. Deer and — and singing birds, and birds like chickens — are all familiar. And dogs."

"Cows and horses?"

"Horses, yes. But I'm sure I never saw a creature quite like a cow before, or machines like planes and automobiles. Of course, the *idea* of all those machines is familiar, and some of them seem familiar, like space-ships, and —"

"*Spaceships?*"

Mary Bean said, "He saw some drawings of space-ships in one of the magazines."

"But I've never been in one," Little Jon hastened to say. "It's just that I feel I've seen them. They are not strange like — like snakes and cows and — and the language you speak."

Thomas Bean sat down. He began snapping his fingers, his face blank. Speech seemed to have deserted him.

Mary laughed. "You wanted facts, Mr. Sherlock

Holmes Bean. We'll toss a couple more at you. Jon, show him your knife. I'll get the clip."

The clip was gold filigree, set with a blue stone. The knife, which had been entirely hidden by its woven sheath, was small, with a short, thin blade that looked like gold. Its handle was of finely carved wood, with a blue stone set in the golden hilt.

"Well?" said Mary, after Thomas had been examining the articles silently for several minutes. "You've been around, Mr. Bean. You're supposed to know something of gems and jewelry. Where were those things made?"

Thomas shook his head. "I've never seen such work. If these stones are real — but of course they can't be. Star sapphires like these . . . h'mm." He picked up a sliver of wood from the fireplace and sliced it with the knife. "Sharp as a razor! Must be a special gold alloy."

Suddenly he stood up. "Let's go down to the shop. I'd like to test these stones."

As they went down the lane, Little Jon heard Rascal bark, and was aware of the eager question in it. *Soon,* he called to Rascal. *I have not forgotten.*

He watched Thomas unlock the shop door, and followed him inside. "Why do you keep the door — locked?" he asked, peering curiously and with quick interest at the rocks cramming the shelves and heaped in the corners, and at the glass case full of gems.

Mary said, "Locks are to keep out thieves."

"Thieves? Thieves?" It was another new word with a confusing thought behind it.

"A thief is a person who steals," she explained. "We have a lot of valuable things here in the shop. If the windows weren't barred and the door didn't have a good lock on it, somebody would break in and take everything we own — even the safe, probably."

"B-but why — "

Thomas asked, "Don't people steal where you're from?"

"Of course not! Why would they? It seems so stupid. They — "

"Go on!" Mary urged. "You're remembering."

"I — " He shook his head. "I almost thought of something, but it's gone. I only know that stealing is — stupid and foolish. I'm sure I've never heard of a person doing it. Why would he?"

"It's one way to make a profit — " Thomas began dryly, "if you don't mind risking jail. There are people who'll do anything for money. They'll even start a war."

"Profit? Jail? Money? War?"

"Here we go again!" said Mary. "You see, Thomas, English *is* strange to him, because it contains *ideas* that are strange."

Little Jon listened carefully, holding back his astonishment as she proceeded to explain. One subject led to another. She had finished about war, and was touching upon government and rulers and power when they were interrupted.

A man on horseback was approaching. It was the same rider who had gone by on the road Saturday evening, before the Beans appeared in their truck.

"That's Angus Macklin," said Mary. "He lives up the road beyond the Johnsons. I hope he goes on."

But Angus Macklin, seeing the door open, stopped, dismounted, and came in. He was a short, thick man with round, blinking eyes and an easy smile. Little Jon was not deceived by the smile, though he was fascinated by the repulsive wad of tobacco Angus was chewing.

"Howdy, folks! Howdy!" Angus said heartily. "See you're open for business. Ought to be gettin' some customers if the weather holds."

"Little early for tourists," Thomas told him. "How are things, Angus?"

"So-so. Ain't seen Tip an' Lenny around, have you?"

"Not this morning. Why aren't they in school?"

"Aw, you know kids," said Angus Macklin. "School's out tomorrow, an' it's kinda hard to make 'em go. When they heard about that wild boy, they just took off. Gilby told me about it yesterday after church. Soon's we got home, my kids lit out to hunt 'im. They lit out again this morning — pretended they was going fishin', but I know better. Mighty queer about that

47

crazy wild boy. Gilby tell you how far he jumped? Near forty feet!"

"Nonsense!" Thomas said shortly. "Gilby was probably drinking. I'm sure he saw a stray Indian kid."

"Oh, I dunno," said Angus, scratching under his cap and blinking owlishly at Little Jon. "That thing he saw was plumb wild and unnatural. I've seen some queer things myself in these mountains. Lights, where there shouldn't be no lights. Heard music where there shouldn't be no music. My kids can take care of themselves, but all the same, that wild thing could be dangerous." He paused. "Nice-lookin' boy you got here. Ain't noticed him around. He visiting you folks?"

Thomas nodded. "Jon O'Connor. Son of an old friend of mine in the Marines."

Angus smiled meaninglessly, and grunted. "Well, I'll go along. You see them fool kids o' mine, tell 'em I want 'em home."

They watched him ride away. Thomas said, a little angrily, "So, the news is out. I should have known Gilby would tell somebody like Angus. It's going to spread all over the mountains, and get wilder."

He drew forth the knife and clip he had hidden under the workbench. As he studied them again, he began to whistle softly through his teeth.

"Out with it," said Mary. "Are the gems real?"

"They're real. I can't quite believe it. Jon, have you any idea what these things are worth?"

48

Little Jon looked at him intently. "They are not worth what you think they are, Mr. Bean. You're thinking they're worth more than your house, and everything in the shop — but that's all wrong. Anyway, a thing shouldn't have two values."

"*Two* values?" said Thomas, raising his eyebrows.

"Yes, sir," he said seriously. "You're judging the value of my knife by the amount of money you could sell it for. But that has nothing to do with its real value."

Thomas whistled softly. "I can't figure you out, Jon. It's a good thing we're not in business together, or we'd never make a profit."

"But — doesn't the idea of a profit seem wrong?"

"I'll try to explain, Jon," Thomas said very patiently. "If Mary and I couldn't make a little profit on the things we sell, we'd soon go broke and wouldn't have enough to eat."

Little Jon looked at them helplessly. Again the dreadful feeling of lostness poured over him. He was sure of the answer now. Mary Bean had guessed it.

Suddenly he turned, peering out of the back window as he heard Rascal barking. Rascal was lost too, chained in a world where everything seemed wrong.

"Please," he begged, "may I take Rascal out of his pen? I promise he'll be good."

Thomas frowned, but Mary said, "Let him try it, Thomas. I'm sure he can manage Rascal."

49

"Um — O.K. We'll chance it this once. And here's your knife, unless you want me to keep it in the safe. You don't want to lose anything like this."

"Oh, I won't lose it, sir. I'll need it to — to — "

"Go on," Mary said quietly. "You need it to — to do what with it?"

"I don't know. Maybe it will come back if I run with Rascal. I think running will help."

As he darted out the door, Mary said, "He's upset, Thomas. I think he sees the truth. Can't you see it too? You've got facts enough — or is it that you just don't want to face the facts?"

"But, Mary, they don't make sense. I can't — "

"Look at him!" she gasped, staring through the rear window. "Thomas — *look!*"

In his eagerness to release Rascal, Little Jon was racing up the steep lane. Unconsciously he had made his feet light, so that his boots hardly touched the ground. Only a deer could have equaled his upward bounds.

"You win," Thomas said finally, expelling a long breath. "I don't know how he got here, and I can't understand why some things are so familiar to him — but he didn't come from this world."

"Of course not. What are we going to do?"

"H'mm. Seems like the important thing is to find out *how* he got here, if we can. I'm afraid I see trouble ahead."

He Remembers Something

Sleep did not come easily that night. For a long time Little Jon lay motionless beside Brooks, thinking of the day while he listened to the sounds beyond the window — the familiar and unfamiliar sounds of a world he didn't belong in.

Somehow, by some accident, he had been lost on a planet that was not his own. It had been hard for the Beans to admit that to him, but of course there wasn't any other answer. Only, how did he get here — and why did so many of the wild creatures seem familiar?

Thomas had a theory about the wild creatures, and life on other planets. As they puzzled over it that afternoon, Thomas had said, "The latest belief among astronomers is that our Earth wasn't made by chance.

It's the result of certain exact conditions. There are other suns just like ours, and the same laws affect them. So there are bound to be other worlds like ours — with life developing on them in almost exactly the same way. If there are people like Jon on them, then naturally — "

"I won't dispute you," said Mary, "but that doesn't solve Jon's problem."

That was when Thomas suggested they get some help.

"Oh, good heavens, no!" she exclaimed. "How could anyone really help us? You know how people are. Don't you realize what a mess it would be if officials started buzzing around? The papers would get it, and we'd have reporters and half the world swarming all over the place. Honestly!"

"Um — guess you're right. Thank Pete some idiot like Angus Macklin didn't find you, Jon. It was lucky we happened on you when we did."

"No, it didn't happen that way, sir. I picked you." He explained to the Beans how he had waited for them.

"That settles it," said Thomas. "If you picked us to help you, we're sticking by you. Now, here's the crazy thing to consider: Our civilization is pretty advanced — the most advanced on Earth — yet we're just beginning space travel. We're not able to reach distant planets yet. So — how did you, whose civilization seems to be behind ours, ever reach us? You must have — "

"Thomas," Mary interrupted, "you're starting off wrong. Can't you *see* how wrong you are?"

"But, Mary, I'm judging by what I see. Jon's people haven't progressed beyond barter and the hand-loom. They must be tribal, for he knows nothing of money, laws, cities, and government."

"Thomas, cities come and go. Governments fall, and money becomes worthless. Is there a mill on this earth that can produce anything as wonderful as Jon's jacket?"

"Well, if we had that kind of fiber — "

"But we haven't. Can anyone on this earth learn a language as quickly as he learned ours — and read our thoughts the way he does?"

"No."

"Can anyone *move* the way he does?"

Thomas shook his head, his lips compressed.

"Thomas," she went on, "if all the people on this earth — everybody — were *absolutely* honest, would we need laws and jails — and armies and bombs and things?"

"H'mm. Guess not."

"Doesn't it seem obvious that Jon's people are actually *far* in advance of us?"

"They're certainly mighty intelligent . . ."

"So intelligent that they could easily have all the

53

expensive and complicated things we have, if they wanted them. But they must not want them. They don't value them. I'm sure they've progressed way beyond them — and value other things more. Thomas, how long do you think it will take us to do away with crime and war?"

Thomas Bean shook his head. "At the rate we're going, we'll need another million years."

"Then there's our starting point. If Jon's people are a million years ahead of us, they've long known about space travel, and they've simplified it. They seem to have simplified everything else. My goodness, Thomas, they could have worked out something as simple as stepping through a door from one room to another."

"That sounds a little farfetched," said Thomas. "But maybe I'm a million years behind. Does it make any sense to you, Jon?"

Something moved in his mind. "From one room to another," he repeated. "Door — door — It seems familiar — the idea, I mean."

"Think!" Mary Bean urged. "Think hard!"

It was no use. The thought, whatever it was, remained in hiding.

When Brooks and Sally came home from school, he spent the rest of the afternoon helping Brooks in the garden. Already they had begun to accept him as Jon O'Connor.

Lying awake in the night beside Brooks, he searched

again for the hidden thought. It seemed important, the most important of all the hidden thoughts; but the harder he searched for it, the farther it seemed to retreat from him.

He dozed finally, and long later awoke suddenly. Rascal was barking, warning of wild creatures crossing the pasture. Deer.

Instantly, silently, he was out of bed, telling Rascal to be quiet while he drew on his clothes. In another minute he was outside, running with lightened feet to the pasture fence and bounding over it.

But the deer had been frightened by Rascal's barking. They had gone back up the forested slope, and refused to come down again.

Disappointed, Little Jon paused, and automatically glanced upward.

For the first time since his arrival he saw the wonder of the stars. Here in the open pasture, above the black bowl of the surrounding mountains, they blazed in uncounted millions. Even as he stared at them, one streaked like a flaming jewel across the sky.

A shooting star! There had been shooting stars when — something happened. Shooting stars — and a door.

He raced back to the house, excited. It was nearly dawn, and the Beans were already stirring. As he burst into the living room he saw Thomas, still in pajamas, lighting a fire in the fireplace.

"There was a door! I remember that part . . ."

"A door?" said Thomas, as Mary hastened in from the kitchen. "What kind of door?"

"I don't know. But it seems that I was standing somewhere, looking at the stars, and I fell. And as I fell, I remembered something about a door . . ."

"Go on," Mary urged.

"That — that's all I can remember, as if it were part of a dream. Just stars, and thinking of a door."

"Could you have been in a ship?" asked Thomas. "You might have fallen out of one in some way."

"No — no — it wasn't like that. I suddenly fell *into* something — and when I woke up I was here on a mountain, and it was morning."

Thomas stood snapping his fingers, frowning. "Mary," he said finally, "it's possible you've hit on the right idea. Jon, as soon as we've finished the chores and had breakfast, we're going hunting. I want to see that spot where you found yourself."

After breakfast, Brooks and Sally went down to catch the school bus, and Thomas got out a knapsack for Mary to fill with lunch. When it was ready he thrust an odd-shaped hammer into his belt and started for the truck.

Little Jon looked curiously at the hammer. "That tool — it seems familiar. Do you — chip rocks with it?"

"It's a rock hound's hammer, Jon. Thought I'd take it along and examine a few ledges while we're out.

Might find a thing or two for the shop. How did you know what it's for?"

"I had the feeling I knew how to use it. Have you another I may take?"

"Why shore, podner, we'll jest go prospectin' together."

Thomas found a second hammer, and they were returning to the truck when a car with a star on the side turned into the driveway. The car stopped behind them, and a lean gray-haired man got out.

At the sight of him, Little Jon was aware of sudden worry and alarm in Mary Bean, who stood watching from the steps. The man approached, studying them carefully with his hard, observant eyes. His nose was slightly hooked, and he made Little Jon think of a hawk he had seen the day before — a hawk searching for prey.

"Mr. Bean?" said the man, in a grating voice. "I'm Deputy Anderson Bush, from the sheriff's office." Hê opened his coat and showed a badge.

"Glad to know you, sir," Thomas said easily, extending his hand. "I've seen you around, but . . . This is Mrs. Bean, and my young partner here is Jon O'Connor. What can we do for you?"

"Like to ask a few routine questions, if you don't mind."

"Sure. Fire away."

Deputy Bush said, "Where were you people Saturday?"

"In town most of the day. Er, is anything wrong?"

"We'll get to that. I understand you have two children. Were they with you?"

"Yes."

"All the time?"

"Well, most of the time, except when they were in the movies. I knew where they were all the time, if that's what you want to know."

The deputy wrote something in a notebook, then looked down at Little Jon. "What about this boy?"

"He didn't arrive until Saturday evening."

"Where was he before that?"

"Traveling — on his way here."

"His parents bring him?"

"No." Thomas lowered his voice, and added, "Both Captain O'Connor and his wife were killed recently, and Jon's been pretty badly upset. Must we . . ."

The deputy finished writing in his notebook before he spoke. "Mr. Bean, I only want to know where the boy was all day Saturday and Sunday. That goes for your boy too. I believe Brooks is his name."

"Yes. You see, this is Jon's first trip to the mountains. Took him all day to get here. He arrived about suppertime. Sunday, he stayed home with Mrs. Bean, and I took my kids to church."

"And Sunday afternoon?"

"We were all here. No one left the place. What's this about?"

Deputy Bush made some more entries in his book. Again he glanced sharply at Little Jon. "Mr. Bean, have you heard anything about a wild boy in this part of the mountains?"

"Er — yes, I have," Thomas replied slowly. "Gilby Pitts told me about it, but I'm afraid I don't take much stock in it. Do you?"

"Mr. Bean, I don't know what Mr. Pitts saw, but it seems to be very unusual. My job is to check up on it. Have you noticed any strange boy around?"

"I certainly haven't seen any boy that looks wild to me," Thomas answered, smiling. "Is he accused of any crime?"

Deputy Bush carefully closed his notebook and returned it to his coat pocket. "No one," he said, "is being accused of anything yet. Do you know the location of Dr. Holliday's summer place?"

"Of course. Dr. Holliday is an old customer of mine. Gilby Pitts takes care of the place while he's away. What about it?"

"Someone broke into it — either Saturday or Sunday. Mr. Pitts didn't learn about it until yesterday morning when he went over to finish some work he'd started last week. Some things were stolen."

"And you think a boy did it?"

"No question of it. There are footprints and other

signs. It was a boy about the size of this one, for he squeezed through a narrow window that a larger person couldn't have entered. He may have had a helper. Now, Mr. Bean, don't take any of this personally; I have to check on every boy in the area. Thank you for your help. Good day, sir."

"Good day, Mr. Bush."

Thomas stood snapping his fingers after the deputy left. "Of all the things to happen!" he burst out angrily.

"Thomas," Mary began worriedly, "do you think it likely that Anderson Bush could find out the truth about — about this wild boy thing?"

"He certainly could! He's no fool. I've never talked to him before, but I know his reputation. He's a born ferret and a stickler for the law — that's why he'd sure give us trouble. Bush doesn't like kids, and he never makes any exceptions. He sure had me going with those questions. If only he doesn't get too curious about Jon and start asking more . . ."

"There's really no reason for him to," Mary said. "It shouldn't be hard to find out who broke into the Holliday place."

"Oh, he'll find out — but that's not what worries me. It's pretty obvious who did it. Only, he doesn't know certain people like we do — he hasn't been here long enough. It'll take time to narrow things down and find out who's lying. And they'll lie. Oh, confound that fool Gilby for bringing up that tale."

"But he had to, Thomas. After all, when there's been a robbery . . ."

"Oh, I suppose so. Well, the thing's happened, and there's nothing we can do about it." Thomas sighed and turned back to the truck. "Let's get on with our hunting, Jon."

He Is Recognized

THE TRUCK wound down toward the lower valley, and stopped briefly at the spot where Little Jon had crouched in hiding on Saturday.

"As nearly as I can guess," Thomas told him, "you must have walked ten or twelve miles through the mountains to come out here. That's all National Forest. You were heading east most of the time. Which way did you head earlier when you were following the deer to that field of Gilby's?"

"I don't know, sir. We wound around a lot. And we went over one low ridge before we got down into the valley."

"H'mm. Have you any idea how long it took you to reach the field?"

"It's hard to judge, sir. You see, I hadn't learned to

count the time the way you do. And I felt so bad — it was all I could do to keep up with the doe. It may have been an hour, or even more. How far can you walk in an hour?"

Thomas chuckled. "In *this* country there's no telling. But let's say you walked a mile and a half, and mostly in an easterly direction. Gilby's place is in a pocket where the valley curves — and it isn't the same valley as this one. So what we'll do is drive past his land, and hike up the mountain to the first cove. If we can't find a spot you recognize, we'll come back tomorrow and start in below Gilby's."

The truck moved on, going up and down and winding in many directions. Finally it crossed a bridge and turned into another valley. They drove past a farm, and several summer cottages that faced a noisy creek bordering the road. The next farm was nearly hidden by the dense growth of poplars along the fence.

"That's Gilby's place," said Thomas, jerking his head as they went by. "Dr. Holliday's property is about a quarter of a mile farther on. We'll stop between the two."

At the first wide spot in the road, the truck was run as far over to the edge of the creek as possible, and they got out. "There's no bridge near," Thomas told him. "We'll have to wade."

"I'll jump," said Little Jon, and without thinking he made his feet light and cleared the stream in a bound.

Turning, he saw the expression on Thomas Bean's face. After Thomas had splashed awkwardly over, Little Jon said apologetically, "I — I forgot. You're afraid someone might see me do that."

"I'd hate for Anderson Bush to catch you at it."

Thomas stamped water from his boots, and squinted at the forested slopes rising on three sides of them. "By the roads, we're nearly fifteen miles from home. Bet you can't tell me in what direction home is — and no fair peeking in my head for the answer!"

"I already know the answer," Little Jon told him, pointing instantly to the south. "It's a short distance over the ridge yonder. You see, I've been watching the way the roads and the valleys curve."

"I'll be jiggered! There's not a man in a hundred would guess that, unless he'd been raised around here. It's only two miles through a gap back of the Holliday place — if you know the trail."

"Oh!"

Thomas Bean frowned at him. "What's worrying you, Jon?"

"I was wondering why Mr. Macklin's boys would steal — and why Mr. Macklin would let them."

"Great guns, how'd you ever get such an idea?"

"Well, you've been *thinking* they did, and Mr. Macklin *knows* they did, because yesterday when he stopped at the shop *he* was thinking about it." Little Jon paused, and looked up earnestly. "Please, Mr. Bean,

64

you mustn't believe that I'm always looking into other people's heads. It isn't — " He groped for a word. "It isn't polite, or even right. The only reason I've been doing it is so I could learn. I *had* to do it. And sometimes you have thoughts that are so strong they — they seem to jump out at me. It goes with the way you feel. It was that way with Mr. Macklin. Yesterday he was thinking about his boys carrying things over the gap, from a house on this side. It didn't mean anything to me then, but now I understand why the thought was so strong."

"Good grief!" Thomas muttered, staring at him. He began snapping his fingers. "What a thing to know — and we can't say a word about it."

He gave a worried shake of his head, and adjusted the knapsack over his shoulder. "Let's forget about the Macklins, and see if we can find that spot we're after. It's getting more important all the time." He thrust through a tangle of laurels, and began limping up a narrow ravine that opened through the trees.

Little Jon followed him easily. He could have climbed twice as fast, had Thomas been able to manage it. It was too bad, he thought, that people here couldn't make their feet light and save themselves so much trouble in getting around. It was such a simple thing. A way of thinking. But it was like so many other things that should be simple — like agreeing on something that was right, instead of trying to make it right

65

some other way. That was why Thomas Bean limped. It had happened in a place called Korea, Brooks had said. Many men had died in Korea — and still no one agreed.

They topped the first ridge, and Thomas Bean stopped to rest. "See anything around here that looks familiar to you?"

"I don't believe I came this way," he said, studying the shadowed cove below them. "If I'd felt better Saturday, I'm sure I could have remembered everything exactly. But my head hurt, and I was so confused . . ."

"Don't apologize. This isn't going to be easy. I've known people to be lost for days in these mountains — and all the time they were within a half hour of a road. Let's start working east."

They followed the cove, crossed another ridge, and tramped for a winding mile or more through dense forest. By noon Little Jon had seen nothing he recognized. Finally they sat down on a mossy outcropping of rock, and Thomas opened his knapsack. Little Jon had finished a sandwich and an apple when he suddenly whispered, "The doe — she's near!"

All morning he had known that many wild creatures had watched them from a distance, and several times he had seen deer go bounding away. He had not tried to call to them. But aware of a friend, he spoke silently, urging her to come nearer. She refused.

66

"What doe?" Thomas whispered. "I don't see —"

"She's way up yonder to the right — the one I followed Saturday. She knows me, but she won't come out. She's afraid of you. Mr. Pitts shot at her and hurt her — it wasn't a bad hurt because I spoiled his aim — but it makes her very afraid."

Thomas growled under his breath, "Had an idea something like that happened. I'd like to wring Gilby's neck."

"I couldn't tell you at the time — I didn't know the words. Anyway, we're getting close, Mr. Bean. The doe proves it."

"But I don't see how. These deer range for miles over the mountains."

"Yes, but she has a fawn that can't travel far, and she's still on the trail she used Saturday, only higher up. There are some — some vines she eats when she can't get anything else."

"Wild honeysuckle. Do you know the direction of Gilby's land from here?"

"Of course. It's straight over yonder." Little Jon pointed. "But we'll have to go way around, then curve to the left."

"Let's get going! I don't know how you keep these directions straight, but with a head like yours, I suppose . . ."

They found the doe's trail easily, and now Little Jon led the way. For Thomas Bean the next half hour was difficult. Many times Little Jon had to help him over tumbled faces of rock, slippery with green moss and running water. When they reached better ground, Thomas glanced back and grumbled, "I'm a fair mountain man in spite of my foot — but when we head for home it won't be *that* way."

"We won't have to, sir. The road's much closer from here. We just turn left — north. Oh — I know this place! Yonder's where I first saw the doe."

He darted ahead, suddenly excited, then stopped to look slowly about him, searching.

"Was it here?" asked Thomas, limping over to him.

"It must be. It's where — no, there was a spring. I drank from it. After that I crawled . . ."

"There are springs all around here. You say you crawled — from where?"

"It was from a sort of dark place."

"You mean a cave?"

"It must have been. I hadn't realized till now — but there's no cave here."

"Let's try higher up," said Thomas, starting upward through a tangle of rhododendrons. "There seems to be a ledge . . ."

There was a ledge. And there was a break in the strata, marking what seemed to be a shallow cave behind the tangle. Near the mouth of it water trickled into a small pool.

"This is the place!" Little Jon cried. "I drank from

the spring — see the marks of my hands? I woke up in there, where it's flat."

They crawled inside. Thomas Bean took a flashlight from his knapsack and sent the beam slowly about. The cave was much larger than it had appeared from the entrance.

"There's been a fall of rock in here recently, Jon. Funny-looking stuff. Looks igneous — but only on one side."

"Igneous?"

"Volcanic. But no volcano ever melted this." He chipped experimentally with his hammer. "It's what we call metamorphic granite — old, old rock that's changing. And something has seared one side of it, a long time ago. I'll be jiggered!"

Thomas went farther back and straightened up. "This place is like the inside of a bottle. We've certainly found something — but don't ask me what. Think, Jon! Think about that door idea! Could this be part of it?"

"I — I don't know, sir. This place, it makes me feel sort of — tingly all over, as if something . . . but I can't remember."

He was aware of Thomas Bean's rising excitement as he chipped off flakes of fallen rock and examined them. Finally Thomas thrust the pieces into his knapsack, and turned the light on his pocket watch. It was later than either of them had realized.

"Pshaw!" Thomas growled. "Hate to leave — but

it'll be nearly dark when we get back, and there are things to do. We'll return first thing in the morning."

They left reluctantly, their thoughts leaping as they talked of their discovery. As the shadows deepened in the forest, they fell silent and began to hurry. Little Jon led the way, following the doe's trail to the valley. At the fence he turned, skirting Gilby Pitts's land, and went through the woods to the creek.

He crossed the creek as before, though not until he had made sure that no one was around to see him.

The truck was several hundred yards around the bend ahead. They were in sight of it when Little Jon heard a car approaching. It was almost inaudible above the clatter of the creek, yet his sharp ears recognized the sound.

He clutched Thomas Bean's arm in sudden uneasiness. "Mr. Bush is coming," he said. "I — I ought to hide."

"There's no reason to. He's already met you. What makes you afraid?"

"I don't know. Something . . ."

There was no place to hide here. The creek fell away on their left, and on their right the rocky slope rose sharply. And suddenly the car with the star on the side was swinging around a curve.

It slowed as it came near them, and stopped. Gilby Pitts was sitting in the front with Anderson Bush.

"Howdy, Tom," said Gilby, his eyes sliding interestedly over Little Jon. "Heard you had a visitor. This him?"

"Yes. We've been doing a bit of rock-hunting together. How are matters up at Holliday's?"

"Been tryin' to make a list of what's been took. Some pretty valuable things. The Doctor's pet target rifle — he paid over three hundred dollars for it. Then there's some expensive fishin' rods . . ." Gilby Pitts rubbed his chin over his high shoulder and leaned out of the car window, squinting downward. "Them boots . . ."

All at once Gilby was out of the car and stooping swiftly. Little Jon knew what was coming even before Gilby's clutching hand gave his trouser leg a jerk to expose the top of the boot. And he was aware of Thomas Bean's desperate thought, *If you'll just keep quiet, Jon, and not say a word, I'll handle this.*

Thomas said, "What's come over you, Gilby?"

"Them's the boots I seen at your house Saturday night," Gilby Pitts said accusingly.

Thomas laughed. "What of it?"

"This kid was there all the time I was there! You never told me . . ."

"That we had a visitor? Why should I? Jon had had a hard day traveling, and we'd put him to bed. What's got into you, Gilby?"

"Them boots," snapped Gilby. "Ever since I seen 'em there I been wonderin' where I seen 'em before. It's come to me. That wild boy was wearin' 'em!"

71

Thomas laughed again, but Gilby said hoarsely, "You been hiding 'im! You cut his hair an' changed his clothes, but you ain't changed his face. I'd know that peaky face anywhere! This here's the ornery little varmint that done the breakin' in and stealin'!"

"Gilby," Thomas said quietly, but with an inner fury that only Little Jon was aware of. "Take your hands off Jon — and stop accusing him before I lose my temper."

"Hold it!" ordered Anderson Bush, who had already stepped from the car and was standing, frowning, behind Gilby. "Mr. Pitts," he said in his grating voice, "are you absolutely sure this is the same boy you saw the other day?"

"I got eyes!" snapped Gilby. "I'd know 'im anywhere!"

"You would be willing to swear to it?"

"On the Bible!" Gilby said emphatically.

"That's all I need to know." Anderson Bush looked hard at Little Jon, and his eyes narrowed as he turned to Thomas. "Mr. Bean, I'm afraid you haven't been honest with me. You said this boy had never been in the mountains before, and that he arrived at your place Saturday night."

"So I did."

"Why is it he was seen over here Saturday morning?"

"Pshaw!" said Thomas. "This thing's getting ridiculous. Who knows what Gilby really saw over here?"

"*I* know what I saw!" Gilby Pitts cried. "An' — *I know them boots!*"

"You see, Mr. Bean?" the deputy went on, his eyebrows raised. "I'm sure Mr. Pitts is a reliable witness. Those *are* very unusual boots the boy is wearing — and the boy himself is, well, different-looking. I'm sure I'd never forget either the boots or the boy, if I'd seen them before."

"Look here," said Thomas, his voice tighter, "this whole thing started because of a robbery that Jon couldn't possibly have had anything to do with. Are you accusing him of being a thief?"

"Mr. Bean," replied Anderson Bush, with a sort of deadly patience, "I'm only an investigating officer looking for facts. I've run into some very peculiar facts that need an explanation. We're due for another talk, Mr. Bean, so I think you'd better go home and wait for me. I'll be right over as soon as I drop off Mr. Pitts."

He Is Accused

IT WAS NEARLY DARK when they reached the house. Little Jon glimpsed Brooks and Sally running from the barn to meet them, and he could hear Rascal whining impatiently in the enclosure, eager to see him and yet reproachful at being left alone all day. He wished suddenly that he had managed to take Rascal with them. The big dog would have loved it. Maybe, tomorrow . . .

"Remember," Thomas was saying, as he set the brakes and turned off the motor, "if Bush insists on asking you questions, let me think the answers before you tell him anything. He can't make us answer — only a court can do that. But I don't want him dragging us into court."

74

"Hi, Dad!" Brooks called. "School's out today! Yow-ee!"

"Mommy said you'd gone rock-hunting," Sally said eagerly, running ahead of Brooks. "Did you find any pretty stones?"

"A few. Where's your mother?"

"Here, Thomas," said Mary Bean, appearing from around the side of the house. "What kept you so late?"

"Trouble," Thomas said hastily. "We ran into Gilby and that deputy on the way back, and Gilby recognized Jon. Bush is on his way over to ask more questions. Keep Sally and Brooks in the kitchen. Jon, you might stay out of sight in the living room — but close enough to hear. I'll talk to Bush on the porch. Hurry — here he comes."

It was a warm evening, and the windows had been opened. Little Jon, huddled in a chair in the darkened room, heard the deputy's feet on the porch, and Thomas Bean's polite voice offering him a seat.

"Would you care for some coffee, sir?" Thomas asked. "I think Mrs. Bean has a fresh pot ready."

"No thanks," came the deputy's grating reply. "I just want to talk to that boy. Will you get him out here, please?"

"I don't see any real reason to, Mr. Bush. I'll answer your questions."

"Mr. Bean, by your own admission, you didn't see that boy until Saturday evening. How can you tell me what the boy was doing the rest of the day?"

"I know where he was," Thomas said. "I know he's no thief, and I don't care to have him questioned about a matter that doesn't concern him."

"You told me his parents are dead, Mr. Bean. Are you his legal guardian?"

"I have charge of him for the time being."

"Then I gather you're *not* his legal guardian. Will you kindly tell me who is?"

Thomas stood up, and Little Jon could feel the rising anger in him.

"Mr. Bush, the only thing that concerns you is to clear up that theft. You're not going to clear it up by wasting your time here. There are other boys in this area you should be investigating."

"Mr. Bean," said Anderson Bush, in his deadly patient voice, "you're being very evasive. When people are afraid to answer questions, that means they have something to hide. What are you trying to hide, Mr. Bean?"

"I'm trying to protect an innocent boy who's had a very bad experience."

Little Jon could almost see Anderson Bush shaking his head. "You're making a mistake, Mr. Bean. I've investigated all other possible suspects, and checked them out. This boy — this Jon O'Connor — is the only one left who could have done it. He was seen, under very strange circumstances, near the Holliday place early Saturday. He's small enough to have squeezed through that window, and there are prints in the dust that could have been made by his boots."

The deputy paused, and went on slowly. "I realize how you feel, Mr. Bean. It's never pleasant to have anyone connected with you accused of a thing like this. But if it's his first offense, and all the stolen property can be recovered, we don't have to be too hard on him. If you'll just call that boy out here and let me talk to him, you'll save yourself some trouble."

"No!" Thomas said firmly. "I'll not have him questioned! He had nothing to do with this!"

But Little Jon was already coming through the door. Thomas, he realized, could protect him no longer without making things worse than they were. He thrust his small hands into his pockets to hide their unsteadiness, and shook his head at Thomas Bean's silent urging to leave. How strange, he thought, looking intently at Anderson Bush, that people here would want to make life such an ugly sort of game. Somewhere, wherever he had come from, there couldn't be this ugliness, or any of these secret hates and desires that darkened everything . . .

"Now, Jon," Anderson Bush was saying, with a friendliness that Little Jon knew was completely false, "I'm glad you decided to come out and clear this thing up. We don't like to see young fellows like you being sent to reform school. So, if you'll tell me where you put those things you took the other day . . ."

"Mr. Bush," he said, "may I ask you a question, please?"

"You'd better start answering questions instead of asking them," the deputy said testily.

"I only wanted to ask you where Mr. Macklin said his boys were Sunday afternoon."

"You can't blame this on the Macklin boys. The whole family was in town all Saturday, at church the next morning, and at Blue Lake with friends all Sunday afternoon. I checked it."

Little Jon turned to Thomas. "Mr. Bean, do you remember when Mr. Macklin rode by Monday, looking for his boys? Can you tell Mr. Bush what he said?"

"Let me think," said Thomas. "H'mm. He said Tip and Lenny had skipped school and were out hunting that wild boy. Gilby Pitts had told him about it at church. He said —" Suddenly Thomas sat up and snapped his fingers. "I'd entirely forgotten it, but Angus said his boys were away all Sunday afternoon doing the same thing. That means Angus was lying if he said Tip and Lenny were with them at Blue Lake."

In the darkness it was hard to see the deputy's face. But his voice was cold as he spoke. "You have a very convenient memory, Mr. Bean. It proves nothing, and it doesn't explain what this boy — this Jon O'Connor as you call him — was doing when Gilby Pitts caught him Saturday. Just who *is* this boy, Mr. Bean? You've admitted you're not his guardian. Who brought him here — and why is he staying with you?"

"Blast your nosiness!" Thomas exploded. "He's the orphaned son of Captain James O'Connor of the Marines, who was killed in North Africa three months ago. The boy has lost his memory, and he was brought here by regular Marine channels because he needs a quiet place to recuperate. I happen to be O'Connor's friend, and his former commanding officer. Enough of that. The only thing that concerns you is the robbery. If you don't believe what I've told you about Macklin, you'd better go over there and have it out with him!"

"We'll all go over," Anderson Bush snapped back. "Get in the car, you two."

It was less than a half mile up the valley. The deputy drove grimly through the night. Little Jon could feel the coiled danger in him, and he wished Thomas hadn't lost his temper and told the lie. He loved Thomas for trying to protect him, but the lie was a mistake. There were old hates in Anderson Bush, ugly things of the past that made the man the way he was now. Little Jon wished the thoughts were not there to be seen, but they leaped out as strongly as if the deputy had shouted them aloud. Anderson Bush had been in trouble in the army, and he hated all officers because of it. Later there had been trouble over a son . . .

The car stopped with an angry jerk before a weathered farmhouse. Anderson Bush slid out, and they followed him up to the dim porch where a hound backed away, barking.

The door opened, spilling light upon them, and Angus Macklin stood there blinking. As Angus recognized the deputy, Little Jon was aware of a flicker of uneasiness in him.

"Why, it's Mr. Bush!" said Angus, smiling. "Thought you was Gilby at first."

"Are you expecting Gilby Pitts?"

"Yeah. He phoned about that wild boy, said —" Angus stopped, his eyes widening as he saw Little Jon behind Thomas. "Tom, I declare, is that really him?"

Thomas Bean ignored him. "There's Gilby coming now," he growled, as lights swung up the road. "Going to be a nice party!"

The approaching truck stopped behind the deputy's car. Gilby and Emma Pitts got out and came up on the porch. Gilby whispered hoarsely, "There's that boy!" And Emma said, "I want to see 'im — I want to see 'im in the light!"

They followed Angus into the big ugly living room where a single glaring bulb hung from the ceiling. A pinched woman, with her hands wadded nervously in her apron, stared at them from the back hall. Little Jon guessed she must be Mrs. Macklin. He was wondering about the Macklin boys when Emma Pitts suddenly grabbed his arm and jerked him under the light.

She was dressed in overalls just as he had seen her

in the field that first morning. He forced himself to look steadily into her hard pebble eyes, and was surprised to see the sudden dawn of fear in them.

All at once she was backing away, exclaiming, "That's 'im! You cut his hair an' changed his clothes, Tom Bean, but you ain't hidin' what he is! He's that same wild boy, an' there's something mighty queer . . ."

"He ain't natural!" muttered Gilby Pitts.

"He sure ain't," said Angus Macklin, backing away. "I can see it in his face! Anything that runs with wild critters — an' jumps like 'em . . . "

Thomas burst out in angry disgust, "For Pete's sake, Jon's not going to bite any of you — but it would serve you right if he did! Mr. Bush, I'll thank you to settle this business and take us home. We haven't had our supper yet."

"Hold your horses," Anderson Bush ordered. "Mr. Macklin, where're Tip and Lenny?"

"Round the barn somewhere," Angus replied. "They got chores."

Little Jon tugged at Thomas Bean's sleeve and whispered the thing that Angus was worried about. Thomas straightened. "Angus," he demanded, "do those chores take your boys as far over as the Johnson place?"

"How come you say that, Tom?"

"Because we just came by the Johnson place. It's not too dark to see a couple boys crossing your pasture, if you happen to be watching. Couldn't make out what they were carrying — but it's not hard to guess."

The smile had frozen on Angus Macklin's face. "You don't sound very neighborly, Tom."

"I missed too many hams last winter to be in a very neighborly mood," Thomas snapped back, finally sure of his ground. "You told Bush you'd taken Tip and Lenny to Blue Lake Sunday, but you told me they were out hunting that wild boy."

"You heard me wrong! I never said no such — "

"Pipe down!" Thomas' voice had a military ring that made Angus flinch. "I'm settling this right now! Your kids ran off Sunday and swiped that stuff from Holliday's. Lenny went through the window — he's small enough. They thought they could blame it on that so-called wild boy. But with the law buzzing around all day, you got to worrying about having stolen property on the place. So tonight you sent Tip and Lenny off to hide the things near the Johnsons'."

Thomas swung determinedly toward the door. "Come on, Bush. Get your flashlight. We don't need a search warrant for this. I'll bet those things are hidden on the edge of Johnsons' woods. They won't be hard to find."

"You're taking a lot on yourself," Anderson Bush said coldly. "You'd better be sure what you're doing."

Emma Pitts cried, "If you find them things in the woods, it'll be because that wild varmint put 'em there! You've got a lot of nerve, Tom Bean, trying to blame it on Angus' boys!"

"There'll be fingerprints," Thomas reminded her, and limped outside.

Reluctantly, Anderson Bush got a flashlight from his car and they started across the pasture below the house. A mist was settling down from the ridge, making the night darker than it had been. After a hundred yards the deputy stopped.

"Mr. Bean," he grated, "I've heard enough lies for one night. It would have been impossible to have seen anyone out here when we drove by. What kind of trick are you trying to pull?"

Little Jon tugged at Thomas Bean's sleeve. "Over there," he said, pointing into the mist.

The deputy swung his light, and Thomas called, "Tip! Lenny! Come here!"

Two vague forms materialized in the beam of the light. They started to run, then halted as the deputy shouted. They came over slowly, two slender boys in soiled and patched jeans, with something secretive in their knobby faces that reminded Little Jon of Mrs. Macklin. Suddenly he felt sorry for Mrs. Macklin, and for Tip and Lenny.

Anderson Bush demanded, "What are you boys doing out here?"

"We got a right to be here," Tip, the taller one, said defiantly. "This here's our land."

Thomas said, "You were coming from Johnson's woods. Take us back the way you came."

"What for? We ain't been over there."

"You were seen over there. Get going!"

"You never seen us!" cried Lenny. "It musta been that wild boy."

Tip said, "We was coming back from the barn when we thought we seen something out here. Bet it was that wild boy!"

"Get going!" Thomas Bean repeated. "Take us where you hid those things."

There were loud denials. Tip cried, "How you think we gonna find something in the dark we don't know nothing about?"

They were approaching the lower fence. Poplar thickets and brush loomed dimly on the other side. Anderson Bush began moving slowly along the fence, directing his light into the brush. Once Little Jon plucked silently at Thomas Bean's sleeve and pointed. Thomas nodded, and whispered, "Wait. We don't want this to look too easy."

They reached the corner near the road, and the deputy turned back. Now he crawled through the fence and very carefully began scuffling through the brush as he swung his light about. Thomas and Little Jon followed him, but Tip and Lenny stubbornly refused to leave the pasture.

The mist settled lower, and presently it became so

thick that the power of the light beam was lost after a few yards.

Anderson Bush said, "It would take a hundred men to find anything out here tonight — *if* there's anything to find."

"Let me have the light a minute," said Thomas. "I thought I saw something gleam way over in yonder."

Thomas took the light, and guided by tugs of Little Jon's hand on his sleeve, plunged deeper into the woods.

Little Jon stopped suddenly before a clump of small cedars growing close to the ground. There was nothing to be seen until he reached in with the toe of his boot and raked out the butt of a fishing rod.

Thomas whistled softly. "They really had them hidden," he muttered. "Bush will never believe we didn't know where they were. Careful — don't touch anything with your hands."

Thomas raised his voice and called the deputy.

Little Jon watched while Anderson Bush carefully drew two fishing rods, a tackle box, and an expensive target rifle from under the cedars. The deputy remained grimly silent until he had tied the fishing rods and the tackle box together with his handkerchief, and looped the gun strap over his shoulder.

"Mr. Bean," he said at last, "you not only have a very convenient memory, but you and that boy have an exceptional ability to locate things you claim you have no knowledge of. But I'll ask you no more questions. I'll leave that to the court."

"Very well," snapped Thomas, "if that's the way you want to play it. But make sure you check all the fingerprints on those things — and in the house as well."

"You can depend on that, Mr. Bean."

He Is Summoned

Rascal was whining forlornly when they got back, begging for Little Jon to take him out. Little Jon went over and petted him, quieting him with a promise for tomorrow, then followed Thomas into the house. It had been a long and difficult day, and he knew that Thomas was badly upset by all that had happened. That was the worst of it — knowing how Thomas felt, and knowing it had all come about because the Beans were trying to help him.

Tonight, if it would have made matters any easier for the Beans, he would not have hesitated to go away. He could leave his knife in payment for Rascal, and he and the big dog could take their chances in the forest. But it was too late for that. It solved nothing, and it would only make things harder for Thomas.

Sally and Brooks were still eating when they reached the kitchen. They were bursting with questions, but Mary Bean silenced them. "You look beat," she said anxiously to Thomas. "What happened up at Macklins'?"

Thomas told her. "So," he finished wearily, "the cat's about out of the bag. Or it will be soon — if Bush has his way."

"People!" Mary blazed. "Why do they want to make so much trouble? But we'll talk about it after you eat. You two get washed. You're filthy."

They cleaned up and ate silently. Finally Little Jon said unhappily, "I'm awfully sorry about all this, Mr. Bean. I wish I could do something to — to —"

"Sorry? Why should *you* be sorry?"

"Because of the trouble I'm causing."

Thomas sat up. "If there's any apologizing to be done, *I'm* the one to do it. I apologize for the stupidity and meanness of my race. But honestly, we're not all like the ones you've met here. Actually, there are some pretty nice people in this world — only there aren't enough of them. It's the troublemaking kind that keeps all the rest of us on the jump, and makes things the way they are. Maybe nature intended it that way — to keep prodding us so we'll learn faster. I don't really know." He spread his hands. "I wish I knew what Bush is going to do."

"When he left," said Little Jon, "he was thinking

about the Marines, and finding out about Captain O'Connor."

Mary Bean gasped. "Oh, no! That would tie it."

Sally, helping with the dishes, said, "Jon how did you know what Mr. Bush was thinking?"

"I — just knew."

Sally wrinkled her nose at him. "I know how you knew." In a stage whisper, she added aloofly, "*You read minds.*"

Brooks gaped at her. "You're crazy as a hoot owl!"

Mary said, "Sally!" But Sally went on quickly, "Jon can! I've known it since yesterday. It's, oh, lots of little things — like always passing me the right dish at the table before I ask for it." She made a face at Brooks. "*You* didn't know it, smartie. That proves girls are smarter than boys — except that Jon's smarter than any of us. I think it's wonderful. I wish *I* could do what he can."

"Thank Pete you can't," Brooks said with feeling. "Life wouldn't be worth living around here." He stared at Little Jon. "Sally's only kidding, isn't she?"

Thomas Bean said, "It's true, Brooks, but stow that down your hatch and keep it battened." He frowned at Mary. "If Bush finds out about the O'Connors, that's all he needs to know. Fingerprints won't matter. He'll haul us into court, and we'll be forced to tell everything."

Thomas began snapping his fingers. Suddenly he

lurched to his feet. "I'm going to call Miss Josie and arrange a private talk with her. She's the only really understanding person around here, and if she knows the facts ahead of time, she'll — What's the matter, Mary?"

Mary was shaking her head. "I've already tried to get her on the phone. I got so worried while you were up at Macklins' that I had to do something. Miss Josie is away tonight. Tomorrow she's got a busy morning in court, and she's flying to Washington immediately afterward. She won't be back till Monday."

Thomas sat down and began snapping his fingers again.

Little Jon asked, "Who is Miss Josie?"

"She's Mrs. Cunningham," Mary told him. "Judge Cunningham, really. But everyone calls her Miss Josie. She handles all the juvenile cases. Oh, I wish we could talk to her!"

She looked knowingly at Thomas. "Did you have any luck this morning — rock-hunting?"

"Yes. Very good luck. I'm taking Jon back first thing tomorrow. It may help his memory."

"Hey, can I go with you?" Brooks asked. "School's out, and — "

"No," Thomas said firmly. "This is too important. Jon's got to recover his memory. His best chance is to start over there on the mountain where he first found himself. We can't have anyone along."

"It's way past bedtime," Mary reminded them, "and it's been a day. Everybody scoot."

Little Jon awoke to a misty morning, with a threat of rain over the ridges. The rain notwithstanding, he and Thomas set out on foot at daybreak, taking the short cut through the gap that led to the other valley. This time Rascal went with them. To Thomas' amazement the big dog behaved himself, and kept quiet even when deer were sighted.

It started to pour when they reached the cave, but neither cared. There was something to be learned here if they could find it. While Thomas crawled about in the dim interior, chipping experimentally with his hammer, Little Jon sat down and tried to think.

Thomas, glancing at him once, said, "Maybe you'd better not *try* to remember. Sort of let your mind go blank. It might come to you easier."

He did as Thomas suggested. Even being here was exciting. Shadows of thoughts seemed to be crowding into the background of his mind. While he waited for them to take form, he drew out his knife and idly began to carve a twisted piece of root that lay near the cave entrance.

The thought shadows refused to take form that morning, but the piece of root did. When Thomas Bean saw it, the rain had stopped, and the root had become the striking head of a man — a man with a curious cap over his long hair, and one hand clenched under his chin as if he were lost in deep thought.

Little Jon was surprised that Thomas should make such a fuss over it. "But doesn't everybody do things like this?" he asked.

"Hardly. It would take a genius like Rodin to produce such a head. Here, look what *I* found. It was under that fall of rock."

Thomas held out a woven cap much like the one in the carving. Little Jon put it on. It fitted him.

"The cap," said Thomas, "proves — at least to me — that you landed here in the cave. It was probably knocked off when you fell, and covered up. It's a wonder you weren't killed. Anyway, the cap also proves that Mary's idea of the door is correct. You see, something had to happen in here to *make* that rock fall on your cap. It isn't the kind of rock that ever splits and breaks into fragments like this — unless a force as strong as a lightning bolt hits it. Now, there's no mechanism in here, or anything that moves. That means that the door, and whatever it is that makes it work, is on the other side — I mean the distant place where your people are."

He was sure Thomas was right. He wondered, with a longing he could not express, if he had a father and mother beyond the door, and if he would ever see them again.

Thomas said, "Let's get back. I want to show Mary these things."

Mary Bean's blue-green eyes were stormy when they returned.

"It's started," she snapped, before they could show her the cap and the carving. "The phone's been ringing all day. Thomas, did you know we've been hiding a wild boy that spits fire, jumps a hundred feet, and eats live rattlesnakes? That's how the tale has grown. I'd like to choke Gilby — and stuff Anderson Bush down his throat!"

She paused for breath. "That's only the half of it. There was a reporter here about an hour ago. I told him he'd been hearing a lot of nonsense, and that we only had the young son of a friend of ours visiting us. I don't think he believed me, and I'm sure he'll be back, because he wants pictures. He had hardly left when *this* came."

Angrily she thrust out a stiff, folded paper.

"What is it?" Thomas asked.

"A summons! To the juvenile court. Monday morning at ten o'clock."

Thomas whistled. "Bush has found out that the O'Connors didn't have any children. He's sure worked fast! I'll bet he got on the phone first thing and called the Marine personnel office in Washington." He shook his head. "All we can do is keep Jon out of sight — and pray that his memory comes back."

"Did you make any progress today?" she asked.

"Some." Thomas opened the knapsack and took out

93

the cap. He explained about it. "It proves you're right about the door idea — and it tells us some other things." He paused and looked around. "Where are Brooks and Sally?"

"I sent them out to pick wild strawberries, where nobody can see them. That reporter caught Sally in the yard and tried to question her."

"Well, we mustn't let Brooks, Sally, or anyone — even Miss Josie — know about the cave. If it's ever so much as mentioned, the news of it will spread and there'll be a thousand people hunting for it. It'll be torn apart and blasted and the pieces probably sold for souvenirs. But if it's never mentioned, it'll never be discovered. You can walk right by it and not know it's there. We've got to keep it that way. It's Jon's only means of getting back where he came from."

"But how — "

"How does it work? Mary, only Jon's memory can tell us that. We're just guessing, but we figure it's a sort of threshold — a place where you land when you step through from the other side. My compass goes haywire in there, so maybe the earth's magnetism has something to do with it. From the looks of it, it hasn't been used for ages."

Thomas paused, then added, "When you think about it, there's no reason why it should ever be used again — except to get Jon back."

Little Jon asked, "Why do you say that, Mr. Bean?"

"Just this: If your people are as advanced as we believe they are, what have we to offer that they'd be the least bit interested in?" Thomas laughed. "I'll bet they took one look at us, and decided we were best forgotten. They probably thought more of our wild creatures — wouldn't be surprised if they carried some young ones home with them, before we finished killing them all off."

Thomas took the carving from the knapsack.

"Have a look at this, Mary. Jon made it while I was poking around."

Mary Bean studied the carving. She said nothing for a minute, but Little Jon was aware of her amazement, the quick turning of her thoughts, her sudden conviction.

"You — you think it looks like me!" he exclaimed. "That it could be my — father."

"Yes, Jon, I do. It would almost have to be. And being what he is, I'm almost sure I know what he's doing this very minute — he's moving heaven and earth to get that *door* thing repaired so he can find you."

Thomas snapped his fingers. "Of course! Jon's here by accident — and if the door were usable, he'd have been found before he left the cave. There's been no change in the place, so it means the thing hasn't been repaired yet."

Suddenly Mary asked, "Jon, can you write in your language?"

"I don't know. I haven't tried."

"Try it now. It's important. If your people came looking for you, they wouldn't know what had become of you — unless you left a message in the cave."

"But if they are like I am," he told her, "they would only have to call — and I'm sure I would hear them, even miles away. Still, if I were asleep . . ."

He sat down at the table with paper and pencil and tried to remember symbols that might stand for thoughts. He doodled and made marks on the paper, but they were not marks with meaning.

"I'm afraid I've forgotten how," he said.

"But you must know your language," Mary insisted. "Remember the little song you sang the other day?"

"I remember that — but I can't put it on paper. Do you suppose if I learned to write your language, that it would help bring back the other? Brooks was showing me the alphabet the other night, and I can print that already. Maybe, if you'll show me how to make words with it . . ."

The writing lesson was interrupted by the telephone, and later by the return of the reporter.

Little Jon hid in the front bedroom while Thomas spoke to the man. The reporter was not easily turned away this time.

"Mr. Bean," he said stubbornly, "you ought to be glad to get a little free publicity. It'll help your business. You'd be surprised at the people who'll come out to your Rock Shop to — "

"I'm quite aware of it," said Thomas, "and I don't want it. Mrs. Bean has already told you about the boy. I can't help these crazy tales that are going around, but I'd advise you to be very careful what you print."

"But at least you can let me take a picture of him, Mr. Bean. I know there's nothing in the tales, and I'd soft-pedal all that. But he's news, and I could do a nice little human-interest story that would help you a lot here."

"Sorry," said Thomas, showing him the door. "No pictures, please."

"O.K. But there'll be plenty of pictures taken when Monday comes."

"What do you mean by that?"

"Mr. Bean, it's already common knowledge that the boy's a juvenile delinquency case. Of course, we're not allowed to print anything like that — but the wild boy angle is something else. You can't stop news, Mr. Bean — and that boy is *news*. I'll see you Monday, Mr. Bean."

He Goes to Court

It was five days till Monday, and Little Jon dreaded it more each day. The phone rang almost constantly at first. Cars filled with curious people began to creep along the road. To escape prying neighbors, and the probability of more reporters, he and Thomas spent long hours at the cave.

None of this helped his memory.

When Monday finally came, Thomas and Mary took him to the courthouse in the center of town, and tried unsuccessfully to slip through the rear entrance without being noticed. A lurking photographer spotted them. Suddenly two cameras were flashing, and they were surrounded by a small crowd of ogling townspeople. Thomas thrust through into the hall, where they were rescued by a policeman.

"In yonder, Mr. Bean," said the policeman, pointing to a door. "Back, everybody! You know these hearings are private."

"Hey, Mr. Bean," a man called, "can that kid really jump a hundred feet?"

The door closed behind them, shutting out the racket. Thomas, Little Jon saw, had timed their arrival carefully. The others were all present, sitting in a semicircle of newly varnished chairs facing a desk. The small room seemed overflowing with eight other people besides himself and the Beans. As he sat down on one side between Thomas and Mary, he could feel every eye upon him.

Angus Macklin and his two boys were sitting over on his left. Angus was smiling, and Tip and Lenny looked stubbornly defiant. Gilby and Emma Pitts were behind them. Anderson Bush, his hands full of papers, was talking in a low voice to a large, square-faced woman in the corner. With the woman was a long-nosed man in glasses. The man seemed aloof and officious.

Little Jon glanced uneasily at the square-faced woman. She kept staring at him as if he were something unpleasant. Mary whispered, "That's Mrs. Groome. She's in charge of Welfare. The man with her is Mr. McFee, the probation officer."

The door on the other side of the desk opened, and a respectful hush fell over the room. Miss Josie entered. Miss Josie was small, gray, and precise. There was no nonsense about her, but behind her quiet, thoughtful eyes Little Jon sensed all the qualities of a friend.

As she took her seat she smiled quickly at Thomas and Mary. "I've been wanting to visit the Rock Shop again, Thomas, but I haven't had time lately."

Thomas was already on his feet. "Miss Josie," he said, thrusting a folded sheet of paper across her desk, "before this thing gets any more out of hand, there are some points that I feel you — and you alone — should know about. I've jotted them down here."

"Thank you, Thomas." Miss Josie smoothed the paper out on her desk and quietly surveyed the room. "Why are you here, Gilby?"

Gilby Pitts gave a nervous twitch of his high shoulder. "Me an' Emma are witnesses, Miss Josie. I got charge of Dr. Holliday's place where all them things was stolen. An' we seen that wild boy when he — "

"That's enough, Gilby!" Miss Josie's voice had the sting of a whip. "You'll not use that expression in this room. If you are called upon to say anything, you'll stick to facts, and facts only — and you'll not repeat them when you leave here."

She turned to Anderson Bush. "Mr. Bush, I've been back in town for three hours, and I've heard nothing but preposterous gossip about this case. Juvenile cases of this nature are *not* for the public. When children

100

get in trouble, they need help, not foolish gossip and publicity. Yet I find our town full of talk, and the courthouse full of curious people. It's disgraceful and disgusting."

The deputy's face had darkened, but he said smoothly, "I'm sorry, Miss Josie, but the talk had already started before I entered the case. Naturally, when someone catches a strangely dressed boy trespassing under the, er, most unusual circumstances — and then discovers that there's been a robbery . . ."

"Let's not waste time, Mr. Bush," she interrupted. "You were ordered to investigate a simple matter of breaking and entering, and theft — obviously committed by one or more boys. Stick to that, and tell me exactly what you learned about it."

Anderson Bush began. He told of Gilby Pitts's discovery of the forced window in the Holliday house, the small footprints inside, the missing articles and their high value. Then he related what Gilby had told him about catching a strangely dressed boy in the field. The deputy paused, and said, "Dr. Holliday's place is only three hundred yards from the spot where Mr. Pitts caught this boy Saturday morning. It was Monday morning before the theft was discovered, and naturally our suspicions centered on this strange boy. I'd like to read you a description of that boy as I got it from Mr. and Mrs. Pitts, and tell you a few facts about him I've uncovered. He — "

101

"That's unnecessary at the moment," Miss Josie said. "Confine yourself to the theft."

The deputy shrugged. "Yes, ma'am. As I was saying, this strange boy seemed the logical suspect. All the same, I investigated three possible suspects in Mr. Pitts's area, and checked them out. That left only the boys living in Mr. Bean's valley. Now, there's a gap behind the Holliday place, which makes it an easy hike from one valley to the other, if you know the way."

"I know about the gap," said Miss Josie. "I've lived in this country sixty-four years. Proceed."

"Well, on Mr. Bean's side there's only Mr. Bean's boy — and this, er, strange boy he has with him — and the two Macklin boys up the road. I checked out the two Macklin boys. Witnesses prove they were away all Saturday and Sunday, which is the only period the theft could have happened. I also checked — "

"Pardon me," said Thomas. "You are leaving out something, Mr. Bush. I told you Tuesday night what Mr. Macklin told Mrs. Bean and me at the shop — that his boys had been out all Sunday afternoon looking for that strange boy."

Angus burst out, "I never said no such a thing! We were at Blue Lake! We — "

"Quiet, both of you," Miss Josie ordered. "Mr. Bush, did you check a second time at Blue Lake and get the names of those witnesses?"

"I did, ma'am. Mr. Macklin and his family were visiting a Mr. and Mrs. Hinkley all Sunday afternoon. The Hinkleys swear to it."

"Mr. Bush," said Miss Josie, "did you know that Joe Hinkley and Angus Macklin were half brothers?"

Anderson Bush stiffened. "No, ma'am."

"It takes time to learn all these local relationships, and you've been here only five years. Proceed with your story."

"Well, ma'am, as I was saying, I checked out Mr. Bean's boy, Brooks. That left only Mr. Bean's visitor, this boy he calls Jon O'Connor. When I questioned him about Jon O'Connor, Mr. Bean was very evasive. He told me that Jon O'Connor was the orphaned son of Captain James O'Connor of the Marines, who was killed recently in North Africa. He said further that the Marines had brought Jon O'Connor to his house Saturday evening, and that the boy could have had nothing to do with the theft. Yet Tuesday evening Mr. Pitts saw this Jon O'Connor, and positively identified him as the strange boy he had caught in his field. Later Mrs. Pitts identified him as the same boy — the Beans had changed his clothes and cut his hair to make him look more normal —"

"But he's the same sneaky boy!" Emma Pitts exclaimed. "I'd know 'im anywhere. He ain't natural!"

"Quiet, Emma!" Miss Josie snapped. "Be careful what you say in here. Mr. Bush, this is all very interest-

103

ing about Jon O'Connor, but at the moment we are
concerned only with the theft. I understand that the
stolen articles were recovered that very evening when
you took Mr. Bean over to the Macklins'. Tell us about
that."

"Yes, ma'am." The deputy pointed to a table in the
corner. On it were two fishing rods, a tackle box, and
a rifle. "Those are the articles, ma'am. When we got to
the Macklins', Mr. Bean insisted he'd seen the Macklin
boys crossing their pasture, carrying what appeared to
be the stolen things. He also insisted that Tip and
Lenny were going to hide the things over in Johnson's
woods, so they wouldn't be found on their own place."
The deputy paused.

"Well?" said Miss Josie.

"It was a pretty dark night," said Anderson Bush.
"I've got good vision, but I didn't see Tip and Lenny
crossing the pasture. However, Mr. Bean insisted that
we immediately search the edge of the woods. We
started across the pasture, and met Tip and Lenny returning. That struck me as rather odd, and I didn't get
an explanation out of them till later. Anyway, I
searched the edge of the woods very carefully, and
found nothing."

The deputy stopped again, and glanced at Little
Jon.

"Go on," said Miss Josie. "Who found the things?"

"Mr. Bean and that boy yonder did. They found

them in less than five minutes. The articles were hidden far back under a cedar clump where they couldn't have been seen even in daylight. It would have been almost impossible to find them at night unless you knew exactly where they were."

"Were there fingerprints on them, Mr. Bush?"

"Yes, ma'am. The fingerprints belonged to Tip and Lenny. When I questioned the Macklins about it afterward, they finally said their boys had found the stolen articles during the afternoon when they were playing in the woods. They'd taken them to the barn. Mr. Macklin says when he learned about it, he made the boys return the things to the cedars, and hide them exactly as they'd found them. He says he was afraid they might be accused of the theft if they reported it."

Miss Josie asked, "Did you find any of Jon O'Connor's fingerprints on the stolen articles?"

"No, ma'am. But they could easily have been rubbed off by so much handling from other people."

"Did you find Jon O'Connor's fingerprints in the Holliday house?"

"No, ma'am. I did find Tip's and Lenny's prints in there — but Mr. Pitts tells me the boys had been in the house a number of times. The doctor had them do odd jobs about the place."

"I see. Now, what have you learned about Jon O'Connor?"

Anderson Bush smiled. "There is no such person,

Miss Josie. I checked with the Marines. It is true that there was a Captain O'Connor, that he was Mr. Bean's friend, and that he was killed recently. But he had no children."

"Very well," said Miss Josie. "That states things clearly. Thomas, what have you to say?"

Thomas Bean swallowed. "It's true that I lied to Mr. Bush. But I had good reasons. Miss Josie, before I try to explain, I wish you'd read those notes I gave you. They'll prepare you —"

Little Jon clutched his arm. "Please — not yet. Miss Josie," he spoke earnestly, "before you read that, will you let me say something first?"

She nodded. "Yes, Jon. We want to hear your side of it."

Little Jon took a long breath. This was not going to be easy. Because of Anderson Bush, he was forced to say and do certain things he abhorred. But, if only for Thomas' sake, he had to go through with it.

"Miss Josie," he began, "Mr. Bean has been trying to protect me ever since he found me Saturday evening over a week ago. I cannot remember anything that happened before that day. I had been in some kind of accident, for I was badly bruised. And I was frightened, because I didn't know what had happened or where I was — except that I was somewhere on a strange mountain. I followed a doe and her fawn down to Mr. Pitts's field, trying to find someone to help me.

106

Mr. Pitts tried to kill the doe, but I spoiled his aim, and — "

"That's a lie!" Gilby cried. "I never shot at no doe!"

"Gilby," Miss Josie said icily, "hold your tongue, or it will give me great pleasure to fine you. Jon, please continue."

"Mr. Pitts caught me, but after Mrs. Pitts came, I broke away and ran. I wandered all day through the mountains until I came out on the road where Mr. Bean found me."

"Jon," said Miss Josie, "during your wanderings that day, did you find the Holliday house and enter it?"

"No, ma'am. I haven't yet seen the place. Besides, I was looking for someone to help me." Little Jon smiled. "I would hardly have expected to find any help in two fishing rods, a heavy tackle box, and a rifle. I knew nothing about such things at the time, and I couldn't have carried them if I'd wanted to. I needed a stick to walk."

He paused to plan his next move. Over in the corner he saw Mr. McFee, the long-nosed probation officer, whistle softly and shake his head. "I've heard some wild ones in my day," McFee said under his breath to Mrs. Groome, "but this kid's tale has 'em all beat."

"Mr. McFee," Miss Josie said coldly, "keep your opinions to yourself. Jon, you've just told me you knew nothing of fishing rods and rifles. For a boy of today, I find that a very strange statement."

"I'm sure you do, Miss Josie. But it's true. You see — "

"Jon," she asked suddenly, "how old are you?"

"I don't know, ma'am."

She studied him a moment, puzzled, then said, "Well, continue your story."

"That's about all, Miss Josie, except for finding the stolen things. After being taken to Mr. Macklin's house that night, I knew exactly where they were."

Miss Josie raised her eyebrows. "You did?"

"Yes, ma'am. Here is how I knew. Will you think of a number, Miss Josie? I believe it will be better if you think of a large one."

"Very well. I've thought of one. What about it?"

"The number you are thinking of is three million, seven hundred and forty thousand, nine hundred and seventy-six."

Miss Josie opened her mouth, closed it, then sat perfectly motionless while she looked at him. The room had become deathly still.

Little Jon said, "I'm not sure my pronunciation is right. I haven't known English very long, and Mrs. Bean has had so much trouble with people interrupting her lately that she hasn't had time to teach me certain things. Is the number I gave correct?"

She nodded, her lips compressed.

"Do you want to try another number, Miss Josie — or something else?"

"It isn't necessary," she answered, almost in a whisper. "It's obvious, Jon, that you can read my thoughts."

"Yes, Miss Josie. It is very unpleasant to have to tell you this, but the thoughts of everyone in this room are so — so loud right now that they might just as well be shouting. So how can I help but know what the Macklins have done?"

"I don't believe it!" Anderson Bush grated. "This smooth-talking kid is full of more lies than any kid I ever — "

"Please, Mr. Bush," Little Jon said quickly, before Miss Josie could speak, "I'd rather not have to say any more. But if you won't take numbers for proof, I'll have to convince you another way. Years ago you were in the army. You were ordered to drive a truck somewhere. On the way you had a bad accident. You — " Little Jon swallowed. "Must I tell what you did, and what happened to you afterward?"

The deputy's jaws were knotted; his face had paled. "No!" he said hoarsely. "I've heard enough." He glared at Angus Macklin. "What about it, Macklin? Have you been stringing me along all this time?"

"No — no — honest I ain't!" Angus had lost his smile. His hands were shaking. "My boys wouldn't — "

The deputy snapped, "You crazy fool, this kid really is a mind reader! Don't you realize what that means? You can't keep a secret from him. *Nobody* can!"

Emma Pitts suddenly cried, "I *told* you that kid's

109

unnatural! Let me out of here — I don't want nothin' to do with no mind reader!" She and Gilby were on their feet, backing away. There was fear in their faces.

The room was in an uproar. From somewhere in a drawer Miss Josie produced a gavel. She pounded it vigorously on the desk.

"Sit down!" she ordered. "Quiet, all of you!"

When the room was restored to order, she said, "Angus Macklin, I've known you all my life and I happen to remember things about you I'll not mention here. Let's have the truth. Did Tip and Lenny break into the Holliday place and take those things?"

Angus swallowed and nodded. "Y-yes, ma'am."

"Where did they hide them?"

"In the barn at first. Then — then I got to worrying about it, and had 'em take the things over in the cedars."

"I see. You thought all the blame would fall on this strange boy everyone was talking about. Angus, this is a very serious matter. The value of those stolen articles is over five hundred dollars. I want you and Tip and Lenny to go home and think about how serious it is. Tomorrow I have a full day, but Wednesday I want you all back here at ten o'clock, and I'll decide what to do about you. I'm afraid Tip and Lenny are badly in need of corrective measures. You, Angus, could be prosecuted."

She turned and glanced at Mrs. Groome and Mr.

McFee. "Does what I'm doing meet with your approval?"

Mr. McFee nodded; Mrs. Groome started to speak, then nodded also.

Miss Josie said, "All right, Angus. You and the boys may go. Gilby, you and Emma may go. But let me warn all of you not to say one word of what you've heard in this room this morning."

When they were gone, it was Mrs. Groome who spoke first.

"Miss Josie," she began disapprovingly, "I don't know what to make of this boy. He may be a mind reader, but I'm not at all convinced he isn't a delinquency case himself. He sounds entirely too clever to be up to any good. Furthermore, if he's really lost his memory and doesn't know where his home is, he's a Welfare case and I should be the one to handle him."

She looked coldly at Thomas. "Mr. Bean, I think you've taken a lot on yourself. Why didn't you come to me in the first place when you found this boy?"

Thomas said, "Mrs. Groome, I did what I thought was best for Jon. If Miss Josie will read what I've written for her, I'm sure she will agree with me."

Suddenly Little Jon found Miss Josie smiling at him.

He smiled back, loving her. "I think you'll find it easier to understand now, Miss Josie," he said.

He Is Threatened

Miss Josie took a pair of glasses from her bag, wiped them and put them on, and unfolded the paper. It was filled with Thomas' small, neat handwriting, the facts carefully arranged as if he were making an official report. As she read, her mouth opened slightly and she bit down on her lower lip. Other than that, she gave no indication of the shock and astonishment that Little Jon knew she felt.

Thomas had listed all that the Beans knew about him — the way he had learned English, his ability to speak to animals, his strange clothing, his total ignorance of some things, and his familiarity with others. It was a long list, and Thomas had even given the value of the gems in Little Jon's knife and clip. Nothing had been omitted but the cave.

He Is Threatened

Thomas had headed the paper:

Secret — for Judge Josephine Cunningham.

At the bottom he had added:

After exhausting all possibilities, we are convinced that Jon is an accidental visitor from another planet. He is sure of this himself. A few scraps of returning memory give proof of it, and indicate how he arrived and how he may be returned. We are working on that now. Our main problem is to avoid further publicity and give him a chance to get his memory back. Our one fear is that some government agency may learn of his abilities and take him away and hold him for study. We feel this would be a tragedy. Please help us all you can.

Thomas Jamieson Bean.

Miss Josie read the paper a second time. Anderson Bush crossed and recrossed his legs, and Mr. McFee began tapping his fingers impatiently on the table beside him. Mrs. Groome seemed to be swelling momentarily. Little Jon knew she was burning with resentment and curiosity.

Suddenly Mrs. Groome said, "Miss Josie, if this boy — whatever his name is — is a Welfare case, I have a right to know whatever there is to know about him."

Miss Josie ignored her. Before saying anything, she carefully folded the paper and put it in her handbag with her glasses. She looked thoughtfully at Thomas, then her eyes met Little Jon's. He smiled back at her, and knew he had another conspirator on his side.

"Thomas," she murmured, "it's fortunate I've known you as long as I have. You did a lot of Intelligence work in the Marines, didn't you?"

"Yes, Miss Josie."

She turned to Mrs. Groome. "Jon is not a Welfare case," she said quietly.

"But — but of course he is!" Mrs. Groome protested. "He's a lost boy — he doesn't even know who he is."

"He was lost for one day," said Miss Josie.

Mrs. Groome seemed to swell even larger. "Miss Josie, I don't understand this at all. What right have the Beans to keep a boy like this — "

"Jon happens to be visiting the Beans," Miss Josie replied firmly. "That's all that is necessary for anyone to know."

"Well! This is certainly *very* strange. If the boy's parents are unknown, who gave him permission to stay at the Beans'? I think this should be looked into. I also think there should be a medical report on the boy. I think I have a right to insist — "

"Mrs. Groome," Miss Josie interrupted quietly, "I quite understand your feelings about the matter. But much more is known about Jon than can ever be told here. He has every right to visit the Beans for as long as they wish. It is very unfortunate that he happened to be drawn into the public eye when so much depends upon — secrecy."

Miss Josie uttered the last word as if she were touching upon high matters of state. It had an immediate effect upon her audience. Anderson Bush and Mr. McFee blinked, and Mrs. Groome was visibly deflated.

"So I must insist," Miss Josie continued, "that all of you say nothing whatever about what you have learned here — not even the fact that Mr. Bean has done Intelligence work. Your silence is extremely important. There'll be questions, and you can help by making light of this — and saying it was all a mistake. And it was a mistake — a terrible one."

She stood up. "Thomas, I'll be out to see you as soon as I possibly can. Mr. Bush, please escort the Beans outside and keep those foolish people away from them."

It was over, this part of it at least, but the rest of it was just beginning. Little Jon knew that as they started for home. Miss Josie had ordered secrecy from everyone, though not for an instant had she believed no one would talk.

Money was bound to make someone talk. That thought had been in Miss Josie's mind when they left.

He said to Thomas and Mary, "I'm sorry for what happened in the courtroom. But I couldn't think of any other way to solve things."

"You had to do it," said Thomas. "There wasn't any other way."

Mary said, "You certainly gave Anderson Bush a jolt — and the rest of them too. Anyway, you prepared Miss Josie for what Thomas had written. She was able to make up her mind quickly and decide what to do. She's a remarkable woman. I wish we'd gone to her when we first found you."

"That was our mistake," Thomas mumbled. "But we had no idea something like this was going to happen. Now too many people know Jon's a mind reader."

"Oh dear," said Mary. "If the papers ever get it . . ."

"They'll get it. The first reporter that waves some cash under Gilby's nose will learn all about it — with trimmings. The same goes for Angus — in spite of the trouble he's in."

They turned into the driveway at last. It was good to be back, and hear Rascal barking a greeting. Little Jon got out and started happily for the enclosure, then stopped as the kitchen door flew open and Brooks and Sally raced toward them.

Something was wrong. Sally looked frightened. Brooks was angry.

"Hey, Dad! Look what somebody threw on our porch a few minutes ago!" Brooks thrust out a crumpled piece of wrapping paper. "It was folded around a stone."

After his lessons, Little Jon had no difficulty reading what was on the paper. Thomas held it for all to see. Crudely written in large letters were the words: THIS IS A WARNING. GET RID OF THAT WILD BOY AND DO IT QUICK.

He heard Mary's gasp, and was aware of Thomas' sudden fury. "Mr. Bean," he said, before Thomas could speak, "if I stay here, I might be a danger to all of you. Maybe it would be better if I went to — to that place we found. I could camp there with Rascal — "

"No!" snapped Thomas. "This is your home. I'll be hanged if I'll let any weaselly bunch of idiots drive you away from here! Brooks, did you get a look at the person who threw this?"

"No, Dad. Sally and I were in the garden when it happened. We heard Rascal bark, then the stone hit the porch. There wasn't anybody in sight. But a little later I heard a car start up somewhere down by the fork. Did you pass anybody on the road?"

"No. He must have taken the west fork when he drove away, after sneaking up here through the trees. It had to be Angus or Gilby, or a relative. There's a bunch of them, counting the Blue Lake people, and they're all related. And they're all afraid now." Suddenly Thomas laughed. "After Jon's exhibition in court this morning, they all know what he can do and they're scared to death of him."

117

Mary said worriedly, "I don't see anything funny in this, Thomas. Some of those people are moonshiners. They could be dangerous."

"If they threaten us again, I'll have to show them that Jon and I can be more dangerous."

"Daddy," said Sally, "did Jon read minds in court this morning?"

"He sure did, honey. That's why those people are afraid."

Sally laughed. "They'd be more afraid if they knew he came from Mars or someplace, wouldn't they?"

"Sally!" Mary exclaimed. "What ever —"

Brooks said, "I told you it couldn't be Mars, Sally. There's not enough air on it. It has to be a planet like ours. Isn't that right, Jon?"

"I think so," Little Jon answered. "But since I can't remember —"

Thomas was staring hard at Brooks, and suddenly Brooks burst out, "Aw, Dad, stop trying to hide it from us! Sally and I have had plenty of time to figure it out. Why, anybody who can do all the things Jon can just couldn't be from *our* planet! He's too smart."

"O.K., son. You know the answer — but keep your hatch battened on it. Too many things are being learned about Jon already, and tomorrow the papers may be full of it. Before anything else happens, he's got to get his memory back."

Little Jon thought of the cave. He was anxious to

return to it, but it was too late to start and get back before dark. They would have to wait until morning.

Every visit had produced something, if only another carving. He had done three: the head of a man older than the first, and another of a woman who Mary Bean believed was his mother. He hoped so. She was so beautiful, and she seemed so wise. Strange how his fingers seemed to remember things that his mind couldn't. But the thought shadows were always there. Soon they would take form. He was sure of that.

Rain was slashing down in torrents the next morning. Little Jon stared out at it in dismay. Thomas said, "It ought to pass in an hour or so. We'll get ready, and leave the moment it clears a bit."

It was barely daybreak and they dawdled over breakfast. They were hardly finished when the telephone rang.

Little Jon answered it. Miss Josie was calling.

"Jon," she said, "I don't suppose any of you have seen the morning papers yet."

"No, ma'am. Mr. Bean doesn't take a daily."

"Well, I've just seen two, and I'll try to get more. I think we'd better have a conference. Tell Mary I'm inviting myself to lunch. It's the only time I can get away."

In spite of the rain, it was a busy morning. Two cars containing out-of-town reporters and photographers came. Thomas had an unpleasant but firm session with them on the porch. They left the the house, but refused to leave the area. Long-distance calls began coming over the phone. A publishing syndicate wanted exclusive rights to Jon O'Connor's story. A nightclub offered a staggering amount of money for two weeks of personal appearances and mind reading. By the time Miss Josie's little car spun into the lane, Thomas was fit to be tied.

Miss Josie said, "I wish I wasn't in such a rush, but everything seems to be happening at once for all of us. Thomas, look at these."

She spread an Atlanta paper and two others on the table. On the front page of two papers were pictures snapped at the courthouse. Under them were long stories. One was headed: MIND-READING GENIUS DISCOVERED IN MOUNTAINS. Another began: WILD BOY READS MINDS, CLEARS SELF OF THEFT CHARGES. The one without pictures had a two-column box headed: WHO IS JON O'CON-NOR? All the known facts had been printed. These were filled in with highly colored rumors and questions.

Mary gasped. "It's worse than I ever —"

"It's what I was afraid of," said Miss Josie. "And it's only the start." She looked at Brooks and Sally. "How much do they know?"

"Everything," said Thomas. "We didn't tell them — they guessed it."

120

"If they guessed," said Miss Josie, "others will too, in time. Jon, have you any idea how valuable you can be to some people?"

Little Jon was shocked by what she was thinking. "I — I didn't realize that this country has enemies. You believe they might — is 'kidnap' the word?"

"Yes. I'm just looking ahead, Jon. Nothing at all may happen, but we'll have to plan for the worst. There are some smart people in this world, and some of them are very dangerous. You said one thing in court yesterday that didn't worry me at the time, but it frightens me now. Somebody was bribed to tell it; it's in all three papers. Here it is: *'The thoughts of everyone in this room are so loud that they might just as well be shouting.'*"

"Good grief!" Thomas exclaimed. "I should have realized the danger of that myself. Why, there are agencies in our own government that, if they knew what Jon can do . . ."

"Exactly," said Miss Josie. "Thomas, I had a call from my brother in Washington this morning."

"The one in the War Department?"

"Yes. He had just got up; he saw a piece in his paper about Jon, and read that it had happened in my court. He was so curious he phoned me immediately. He was entirely too curious, Thomas, and he mentioned that we might have a visitor." Miss Josie paused, then asked, "Did you ever hear of a Colonel Eben Quinn?"

"H'mm. I once had to deal with a Major Eben Quinn. Tall, thin, very pale. The only thing I'll ever repeat about him is that I'm glad he's not working for our enemies."

"Well, he's a colonel now," said Miss Josie. "No one knows what department he's connected with, but he has power. Entirely too much for a colonel. Thomas, I think we'd better hide Jon. For his own safety, I think we should get him away from these mountains to someplace where he won't be recognized."

Little Jon said, "But I can't leave, Miss Josie. I *have* to stay here."

"Why, Jon?"

Thomas said, "Let me explain. Miss Josie, he doesn't dare leave here, or he'll never get back where he came from. There's a — a connection in this area, something magnetic, that forms his only means of return. He has to regain his memory here, and be close by when his people come looking for him — and from what we've learned, we're sure they will."

"Oh my, this does complicate things." She frowned and looked at Little Jon, and said almost absently, "I wish you had your memory, and that I had hours to talk to you instead of minutes. I must have read what Thomas wrote about you a hundred times last night. It gave me a glimpse of what a peaceful and wonderful place your world must be — and how strange and

122

terrible ours must look to you. Jon, the awful part is what people here would do to you if they could. They'd use you. They'd pay no attention to the good you could give; they'd use your mind to help fight their secret battles. And no matter which side got you, nothing would be changed. It would still go on . . ."

Miss Josie shook her head suddenly. "I've got to think of something. Thomas, there's a legal side to this that worries me. By law, you and Mary have no real authority to keep Jon. Before some agency tries to take him away, I'd better have papers drawn up giving you temporary custody of him."

She stopped and stared out of the front window. "Oh, no! Look at those cars on the road. Silly people coming to gape. This settles it, Thomas. You'll have to have a guard here."

Brooks said, "Miss Josie, I think we need a guard. Look what someone threw on the porch yesterday." He showed her the piece of wrapping paper with the warning on it.

Her face tightened as she read it. "I don't like this, Thomas."

"What can they do?" said Thomas. "One of Gilby's bunch wrote it, I'm sure. They're just scared. Still — " Thomas paused and began snapping his fingers. "After what's in the papers, someone may try to use them. They're fools enough to let some clever person . . ."

"Yes," said Miss Josie. "That's exactly why they're

123

dangerous. Thomas, I'm going to send a deputy out here this afternoon, and try to get another one for night duty. I'm not sure I can manage a night man — you know how our sheriff is: if he smelled smoke, he wouldn't believe there's fire unless it burned his nose. Anyway, I'll fix up those papers as soon as possible."

That afternoon a young deputy drove out, parked his car near the edge of the lane, and stood waving traffic on while he barred the lane to visitors. His presence, however, did not prevent a television truck from stopping under the trees at the far side of the road. Its crew set up a camera on a high platform and began taking pictures of the growing traffic and everything happening on the Bean property.

When the young deputy went off duty that evening, no one came to take his place. He had been gone hardly ten minutes when a stone crashed through one of the front windows. Wrapped around it was a piece of paper covered with another crudely lettered warning: GET RID OF THAT WILD BOY — WE MEAN BUSINESS.

"Where's this thing going to end?" Thomas muttered angrily, as he nailed a board over the broken pane.

He Is in Danger

THE NEXT DAY started badly. They had planned to leave early for the cave, but when Thomas went out to the barn at dawn he discovered that his one milk cow was missing. She had gone back into the pasture the night before; this morning the pasture was empty, and the gate to the road at the far end of it was open.

It was obvious that the cow had been stolen, and most certainly for spite. Little Jon knew that Thomas never expected to see her again. The road was jamming with cruising sightseers, and the young deputy, back on duty, was having trouble keeping a fresh batch of reporters out of the yard.

The deputy had brought Mary a paper from town. There were pictures in it showing the Bean place and

125

the deputy standing in the lane. The story was captioned: MYSTERY BOY'S FAME SPREADS, HOUSE GUARDED. In a separate column a new question was asked: IS MIND READER FROM MARS?

Thomas glanced worriedly at the headlines, and glared at the passing cars through the unbroken window. Little Jon, watching him, was sick at heart. Who would have dreamed that his presence here would cause so much trouble? He was wondering what he could do to repay the Beans when he saw Thomas stiffen.

A long black car, driven by an army chauffeur, had turned into the lane past the protesting deputy. Two officers in uniform got out.

"That's Quinn!" Thomas exclaimed. "If he thinks he's going to see you, he's got another guess coming."

Little Jon peered uneasily at the officers from the corner of the window. Colonel Eben Quinn was the tall, pale one. The colonel paid no attention to the guard. "Official business," he snapped, without turning his head, and strode up to the house as if he owned the world.

Thomas met him on the porch.

Colonel Quinn was very pleasant at first. He shook hands with Thomas, introduced his aide, a Major Gruber, and said how delighted he was to see Captain Bean of the Marines again. It was all surface talk, Little Jon knew, for the colonel was far from pleased with the thought of having to deal with someone like Thomas.

"My department," the colonel said finally, "is much interested in Jon O'Connor. Aren't you going to invite us in to meet him?"

"No," said Thomas. "I am not."

"You are being very inhospitable, Captain Bean."

"Sorry," said Thomas. "I'll have to remain inhospitable."

"You are not acting wisely, Captain. I understand the boy has lost his memory. We have some fine doctors in Washington. We'd like to help that boy . . ."

Thomas' voice hardened. "Tell me another tale, Colonel. I know exactly what you want with him. You'll not have him."

Colonel Quinn suddenly chilled. "We'll see about that. Are you his guardian?"

"I am," said Thomas. It was stretching a point, for Little Jon knew Miss Josie had not yet prepared the papers.

"I doubt it," the colonel snapped. "I had a talk with Mrs. Groome before I came out. She's of the opinion that Judge Cunningham has been exceeding her authority in the case of Jon O'Connor. The whole matter is very curious, and we've been investigating it. The fact remains that nobody knows where Jon O'Connor came from, and no one can claim him. But the government has a certain priority."

The colonel paused. Little Jon was aware of Mary standing close; now he felt her hand on his shoulder, tightening. Brooks and Sally had crept nearer, and Brooks was thinking, What right has that tall guy got to come here and try to take Jon from us?

"Under the circumstances," said Colonel Quinn, "I think you would be wise to consider our proposal. Jon O'Connor has a rare gift we can use. In return we will give him the best of homes and care — anything he wishes, in fact. If the boy wants you and your family with him, I'm sure that can be arranged."

"No," said Thomas, turning away. "You're wasting your time. Good-bye, gentlemen."

"Not so fast," Colonel Quinn said icily. "If you persist in being stubborn, we'll very quickly find legal means to take the boy off your hands."

"Try it," said Thomas. "And I'll fight you with every dollar I've got. Jon has some rights, and I intend to protect him."

"We'll see about that. In the meantime I'll warn you not to let that boy out of your sight. There are others just as interested in him as we are. You were in Intelligence — you know what they're like. If anything happens to him before we get back, we'll hold you responsible."

Colonel Quinn spun on his heel, and, followed by his aide, strode quickly out to his car.

It was a very grim Thomas who reentered the room.

For long seconds no one spoke. Then Brooks, wide-eyed and half frightened, said, "Good grief, Dad, who'd have thought — I mean, what can we — "

"Yes," said Mary. "What *can* we do, Thomas? This is getting to be perfectly awful!"

"I'd better phone Miss Josie," said Thomas.

It was past noon. Thomas managed to get Miss Josie at her home. While Thomas talked, Little Jon tried to think. Everything was so unbelievably tangled on this world, with their laws and their money and their hates and their fighting for power. He could see only one solution that might help the Beans.

Thomas hung up at last. He shook his head. "Miss Josie's trying to work out something, but all this pub-licity — and Quinn on top of it — has stirred up a hornet's nest. Mrs. Groome is making trouble, and if the government steps in . . ."

"But, Thomas," Mary cried, "they just *can't* take him away."

"I'm afraid they can, honey. If this were Jon's world, and Jon's country, it would be an entirely different matter. And if Miss Josie had more time, and could give us a chance to adopt Jon legally as our son, we'd have some rights. But there isn't time. Quinn wants Jon, and Quinn's going to get him — unless I can hide him somewhere, and fast."

"No," said Little Jon. "I've caused enough trouble, Mr. Bean, I think it would be better for everyone if I go with Colonel Quinn and do what he wants."

"Absolutely not! If Quinn gets his hands on you, you'll never see home again. We're going to that place we discovered. No one can find you there — and it's mighty important that you be there anyway. Mary, get us some blankets while I fill the knapsack. Jon, maybe you'd better change into your own clothes — we've nothing to compare with them for camping."

There was no changing Thomas' mind. In a very short time they were slipping out past the garden fence, carrying their equipment. Rascal trotted beside them.

They edged around the barn, skirted the pasture, and reached the road a quarter of a mile beyond the house. They crouched in the brush until no cars were in sight, then hurried across. In the woods on the other side they began angling up the slope toward the gap trail.

They were still some distance from the gap when Little Jon stopped at a warning from Rascal. "Mr. Bean," he whispered, "we're being followed."

Thomas froze. "It must be reporters," he muttered.

"No, it's Mr. Pitts and — some strangers. Men I haven't met or seen around. I — I should have known about this earlier, but there were so many people on the road . . ."

His mind went out, searching, and his small hands clenched as he became aware of the danger they were
130

in — Thomas especially. They would kill Thomas to get Jon O'Connor. It shocked him to realize that men would place such terrible value on Jon O'Connor's ability.

He said quietly to Thomas. "They've been watching the house with — with field glasses, waiting till we left. They can't see us here, but they saw us cross the road. Mr. Pitts thinks we're heading for the gap."

"If we hurry," Thomas whispered, "we can lose them on the other side."

"No — they've stopped, waiting for others to come. There are four — five in all. Mr. Pitts is talking to them. He's telling them we're bound to get away, once we cross over. He's going back and get a dog — that bloodhound you once had. If the others can't catch us, they'll wait for him at the gap. He — he thinks they're some sort of government men he's helping."

Muscles knotted in Thomas' jaw. "A fool like Gilby would swallow that. They've got us checked. We can't go to the cave. That bloodhound could trail us anywhere."

There was nothing to do but circle back, as quickly and as quietly as they could, and return to the house.

The sun had gone down over the ridge when they finally slipped in through the kitchen door. Mary paled when Thomas told her what had happened.

"You'd better call the sheriff," she urged. "That young deputy has gone home for the night, and Jon's got to have some protection. This is an attempted kidnapping."

Thomas made several calls, all without result. The sheriff was away from town, and there were no deputies immediately available.

"If I know Quinn," muttered Thomas, "we'll soon have more protection than we want. He'll get a company of military police out here and sew us up tight."

"He was thinking of doing that when he left," Little Jon told him.

Thomas locked the doors, and began limping about the room, snapping his fingers. Once he went into the bedroom and came back with a pistol thrust into his pocket. Little Jon knew he hated weapons; Thomas had used too many in the past . . .

Little Jon studied the road through the windows. The twilight was deepening. A knot of coldness gathered in him as he considered what might happen to the Beans. So long as he was with them, Brooks and Sally and all of them would be in danger — unless the military police came, and that probably wouldn't be till morning. Danger was out there; it wasn't close yet, but it would surely come upon them after dark. The road would be clear, and the one remaining car containing watching reporters would be gone.

Already the unknown men with Gilby had discovered that he and Thomas had not taken the gap trail.

He wished he could understand what they were

planning. But they were scattered about, and there were more men gathering. So many thoughts were confusing . . .

Thomas came over beside him. "Jon," he said softly, trying not to show his growing worry, "what's going on outside? Any idea?"

"I'm trying to find out."

It was hard to concentrate. Something was stirring in his mind. He tried to thrust it away, for at the moment it didn't matter. All that mattered was to draw danger away from the Beans.

As he studied the twilight again, he was aware of Rascal's uneasiness. Suddenly he knew that Gilby Pitts was somewhere over on the edge of the pasture, in the shadows. Gilby had Angus Macklin with him, and some of their friends. They were going to help the outsiders, as soon as dark came . . .

What was their plan?

He tried to reach Gilby's thoughts, but other thoughts kept intruding. There seemed to be a whispering in his mind.

Little Jon! Little Jon! Where are you?

All at once he gasped, and stood rigid as understanding came.

Mary, seeing him, cried, "Jon! What's wrong?"

"The Door — it must be open!" he managed to say. "My people — they are here — they are calling me . . ."

He Escapes

"CAN YOU HEAR THEM?" Thomas exclaimed. "In your mind, I mean? They've come for you?"

"Yes — they've come through that place — it really is a sort of door . . . I can almost see it . . . it was broken on the other side, but they've got the power working, and the Door is open . . . it's a shimmering spot, and you step right through it as if space were nothing . . ."

His hands were suddenly trembling; he clenched them and closed his eyes, listening to the silent voices calling eagerly to him. He answered and told them about the Beans and what had happened. *Stay where you are,* he begged. *There is danger here. The Beans are in danger because of me. I must help them.*

He opened his eyes and looked at Thomas, and then

at Mary. "They are over on the side of the mountain, waiting for me. My father is with them, and my mother . . ."

"Oh, Jon, I — I'm so happy for you!" Mary's chin was suddenly trembling; there were tears in her eyes.

Thomas said, in a voice that was not quite steady, "Jon, can you — is it possible — for you to make a break for it now, and reach them safely?"

Little Jon bit his lip. Alone, he could do it easily.

"Yes," he said. "But what about you?"

"Don't worry about us," said Thomas. "We'll be all right."

"But you wouldn't — nothing here would ever be all right. If I disappeared, you couldn't explain what had happened to me. Colonel Quinn wouldn't believe you. Few people would. There'd be all kinds of trouble . . ."

"Confound Quinn! I'll handle him somehow."

"But what of the others?" Little Jon persisted. "The ones out there — could you make them believe it? Don't you see what would happen?"

Thomas turned pale. "I didn't realize . . ."

Thomas knew now. Mary did too. Sally and Brooks would be in danger. They would surely be taken, and held to be exchanged for Jon O'Connor. Life for the Beans would never be the same. There would be questions and trouble for years. Little Jon knew they had no near relatives, no one they could turn to.

And time was getting short. It would soon be dark. They had only minutes to decide something . . .

He looked at them — Thomas, Mary, Brooks, and small Sally with her frightened eyes and brave chin. He loved them all, and he didn't want to leave them.

"I don't remember what it's like where I came from," he told them. "But I *know* it isn't like this. I'm sure, just from listening to what they are saying to me now, that we live in small groups, and help one another. There are not too many of us, but we have great knowledge, and we've made life so simple that we don't have laws or even leaders, for they aren't needed any more than money is needed. I think we make things — everything — with our hands, and that life is a great joy, for we have time for so much . . ."

They were staring at him, and Mary whispered, "Jon, what — what are you trying to tell us?"

"I — I'm trying to tell you that you'd like it there, and that I want you to come with me. I've been talking to my people, explaining what's happened to us, and telling them that I can't leave you. They — they've agreed that you must come with me."

They gasped. He read their sudden confusion. How could they drop everything? . . . They needed time to think, to plan . . .

"There's no time left," he hurried to say. "You won't need anything from here — just flashlights to see your way through the woods . . ."

136

He Escapes

Suddenly Sally said, "Oh, Jon, I think it would be wonderful to live in a place where all the animals were friendly, and nobody hunted them. Please, Daddy — "

"Yes," said Mary. Thomas said, "O.K., Jon. How do we manage to get away from the house?"

"After I leave, wait a few minutes," he told them. "When you hear shouts out in the pasture, get in the truck and drive as fast you can up to the gap trail. Then climb to the gap. I'll meet you up there."

Before they could ask questions he darted to the kitchen door, unlocked it, and raced outside.

He reached the enclosure in two bounds, and released Rascal. *Stay behind me,* he ordered. *Keep quiet.*

Where was Gilby now? His flying feet took him across the garden and over the pasture fence. As he touched the pasture he heard a shrill whistle from the road, and an answering whistle ahead. It was still twilight and he had been seen already. It was better than he had hoped for.

He slowed, pretending to be undecided. In the shadows ahead he could make out Gilby and Angus and several others. He realized that their plan had been to fire the barn and draw attention from Jon O'Connor, who would be left unguarded. But Jon O'Connor was here — and he could see Angus, who carried an oil can, gaping at him in utter astonishment and disbelief, and sudden fear.

There was a quick clattering of shoes over the stones

137

along the edge of the pasture. Other men were coming in a rush.

As he turned to dart away, a man called hoarsely, "Head the boy off! Don't let him get past! Hit him with something — but watch out for that dog!"

A hurled stone went past his head. He leaped easily beyond the frightened Angus, and saw Rascal spring growling at a second figure that tried to block his way. He listened for the sound of Thomas' truck. The way was clear, and the Beans should be leaving . . .

A rock grazed his shoulder, and another struck his back with such force that he stumbled and almost went sprawling. He gained his balance, but too late to avoid the next stone. There was an instant when he saw it coming, and abruptly there was the stunning impact of it across the top of his head.

Consciousness did not leave him as he fell. He heard men shouting, the pounding of approaching footsteps — and a man's sudden scream as Rascal slashed into him. The big dog was all at once a whirling, snarling fury, his charges sending men tumbling as his fangs ripped cloth and flesh.

Little Jon heard all this, but as his hands clutched the pasture grass it seemed for a moment that he was somewhere else — far away on a hill at home . . . Memory flooded over him, and he saw again the valley people on the hill, and the glittering wonder of the shooting stars they had come to watch . . . Then he

138

had fallen into the hill — into the crumbling chamber with its old machine. The machine spun a force that bridged space in an instant. You stepped through the shimmering Door it made — and the threshold on the other side was somewhere else, another world.

He struggled to his knees, aware of the fury that was Rascal, of a man crawling away in pain . . . This wasn't home. This was the strange world, Thomas Bean's world. Only, there were too few in it like Thomas Bean, and the Door to it had long been closed . . .

He heard the sudden roar of Thomas' truck, and he sprang up with a glad cry. This was no longer Thomas Bean's world — the Beans were leaving . . .

He began to run. Behind him Rascal made one final charge, then raced to overtake him. There was pursuit, but his pursuers might have been following the wind. He and Rascal cleared the road together, and went bounding upward through the darkening woods.

He met the Beans on the trail, and led them on to where his people waited. They all carried glowing lights that made a radiance in the forest. But presently, one by one, the lights vanished.

The forest grew still again, and empty save for a wandering doe and her fawn.

The Bean house stands empty. All through the

mountains people whisper of it, and shake their heads. When the first investigators came, there was still food on the table, untouched. Everything the Beans owned was there, and nothing had been taken, even from the shop. Thomas Bean's truck was found up the road, abandoned. The Beans had simply vanished, empty-handed, without the least sign to indicate what had happened. And the strange boy, Jon O'Connor, had vanished with them — leaving an angry and baffled colonel who appeared the next morning, and whose men searched the mountains for days.

So the Bean place stands empty, and the pasture and the fields are overgrown. Gilby Pitts never goes by there if he can help it. Angus Macklin has moved away. Miss Josie went there only once, just after the colonel left. She found three curious carvings on Thomas Bean's desk, which no one else had eyes for. She treasures them, and often wonders about them when she is alone, but she has never mentioned her thoughts to anyone.

Across a threshold, and somewhere far beyond, there is a hill where the valley people often gather when the day's work is done. From it you can watch the glittering night unfold, and see the whole magic sweep when the shooting stars begin to stream like jewels across the sky.

Even the deer come out to watch, unafraid.